To Miloud Achdini and Hassan El Bou who are still living,
and in a twofold way, the ordeal

I dedicate this book.

The title of this work in French is *Le chemin des ordalies,*
first published in 1982 by Editions Denoël in Paris.

© Editions Denoël, 1982

First published in English by Readers International Inc. and
Readers International, London. Editorial inquiries to London
office at 8 Strathray Gardens, London NW3 4NY, England.
US/Canadian inquiries to Subscriber Service Department,
P.O. Box 959, Columbia, LA 71418-0959 USA.

Cover art: Maghreb scene by Riccardo Wolfson
Arabic calligraphy: *Awdah* ("Return") by Mourad Boutros
Cover design by Jan Brychta
Typesetting by Opus 43, Cumbria UK

Library of Congress Catalog Card Number: 88-63241

British Library Cataloguing in Publication Data
âbi, Abdellatif, *1942—*
he du Retour
Title II. *Le chemin des ordalies. English*
3'.914(F)

N 0-930523-64-4 hardcover
N 0-930523-65-2 paperback

Abdellatif Laâbi

Rue du Retou

Translated from the French by Jac
Foreword by Breyten Breyt
Introduction by Victor Re

readers int

MERCYH
HAMMF
ERIE

Foreword: The Seed of Fire
by Breyten Breytenbach

Somewhere in these pages Abdellatif Laâbi writes about "hands with the slow fire of waiting". Maybe I could stretch the metaphor by saying that the book itself is a flame — because it is both the description of an ordeal and its burning away until the essentials are laid bare, a torture and a purification, illuminating a life and transforming it to the light-ness of being, so that the book becomes both the illustration and the incarnation of its own existence.

It is the work of a poet. A poet is arrested (it is clear that he is a political opponent of the régime of his country, Morocco). He is interrogated, tortured, tried and sentenced to a long term of incarceration. To be in prison is to be buried alive. The poet's cell is a tomb. "You live in your cell like a blood-stained sword in its sheath." He writes: letters to his beloved one, poems and stories, dreams and fears and fables. It is not even a matter of choice. A flame is that by virtue of its burning. "Write or be killed," his tormentors threaten. But not writing *would mean being smothered by* history. *Silence is death by default. Inevitably he will grow — "ceilings are there to be passed through," he says — he will write with the deep fire of seeds in the earth, and in due time his writings will be like wild flowers unfolding to ripen and sweeten the sun. He is released and returned to "normal life". Now comes the time of re-adaptation, of measuring the changes and the distances, tasting the unsayable darkness of the tongue. Engraved within him, as a map of the womb, he carries the fortress of iniquity. He is a foreigner to himself, and yet an intimate observer, plotting the course of "the old salt of the prison seas". There is now the urgency to tell, to share the experiences of this voyage — because it is a true one, and therefore illustrating the human fate — before he is sucked under by the swirl of banal freedom. He will be brought face to face with death as mirrored in the wrinkles of exile.*

Fire. Germination. Birth. Blood. All of these themes are burnished and boned image by image until they echo through Abdellatif Laâbi's book. I am but quoting at random. Of course I am flattening its surface by skimming over it in such a cursory way. The ordeal is observed in all its subtle tones and intonations, and described with a richness of detail and incident. The book speaks of patience and of waiting, of loyalty and compassion and comradeship, of despair and resistance and tenderness, of nearness and of distance. We experience the vomited dark scream of the tortured one, we live the death of the mother, we encounter the dankness of prison and we hear the brief wing-beat of prisoners conversing, we taste the cigarette, we fall in love with the sun, we break through the walls of cell and mind. Always Awdah is there, his beloved companion. This is perhaps the core: the sailor/seed/sword/poet, and Awdah who is sister and mother and daughter and mistress — the two of them enfolded in the apparently neutral flickering of light and darkness of the observer's voice. You put the book down and it still rings in the mind; rather, it rings the mind with fire.

Let the book speak for itself. The flame suffers no exegesis. As for Abdellatif Laâbi: he is a free man. Maybe he was always free. (His country is not free, and many people are tortured and incarcerated there. This too needs to be remembered.) His has been the essential human experience — self-discovery through the knowing of the other; and then the essential human gesture — the expression of that realisation of one-ness, of none-ness, and thus (nonetheless) of our shared brotherhood. He speaks to those of us who can still hear man's wild cry of revolt and the madness of his hopes. Hope is a hard task. But he has lit the flame.

Prison constitutes an underground of linked dreams spanning continents and centuries. My African brother, Abdellatif Laâbi, as you will see, is a member of the same cell as Dostoevsky, Hikmet, Soyinka, Cervantes . . . Subversive pyromaniacs all, and fools!

Introduction

On January 27, 1972, Abdellatif Laâbi was arrested at his home in Rabat, Morocco, for "conspiracy against the state", a euphemism for crimes of opinion. Brutally tortured, imprisoned, given a provisional release, then rearrested, he undertook a series of hunger strikes until he was granted a trial in August 1973, after which he was sentenced to ten years' imprisonment. He was released eight and a half years later, following an international campaign mounted on his behalf by Amnesty International, the French branch of PEN and other groups. Key to this effort was his close friend and associate Ghislain Ripault, who figures in this book. For a period of four years following his release, Laâbi was deprived of both passport and work. An anthology of pieces written in his honour and defence by fifty Arab and European writers and artists was published in Paris in 1982, and he was eventually allowed to leave Morocco. Since 1985 Laâbi has lived in Paris with his wife Jocelyne and their three children.

Poet, novelist, essayist, playwright, translator, storyteller and human-rights activist, Laâbi is one of the most prolific and critically acclaimed of present-day North African writers. *Rue du Retour* is the first of his many fine works to be translated into English.

Born in Fes in 1942, Laâbi took a degree in French

literature at Rabat University and, until the time of his arrest, taught French at a lycée in Rabat. With the publication of his first novel, *L'Oeil et la nuit* (1969), and numerous poems later published in the volumes *Le règne de barbarie* and *Race*, he emerged as a leading voice in Moroccan literature. In 1966 he founded the avant-garde literary review *Souffles* (first published in French and subsequently in both French and Arabic) which was to influence an entire generation of writers and intellectuals throughout the Maghreb. He later founded another journal, *Anfas*, published in Arabic. His contributions to both these journals, both theoretical and literary, laid the groundwork for what has become a renaissance in North African literature.

From the outset Laâbi and his collaborators conceived of a new Moroccan literature that would be committed to certain progressive ideals, a literature that would challenge the fettered sociopolitical system in Morocco and the neocolonial values it perpetuated, that would support other repressed peoples (in particular the Palestinians and African peoples), and that would break out of the straight-jacket of literary forms inherited from the West. Laâbi coined the term "itinerary" to identify this new literary form, in which the traditional Western distinctions – between prose and poetry, narrative and discursive, and even oral and written literature – would be eliminated in the quest for new, radically indigenous forms.

The boldness and innovations of the new movement were not long tolerated by Moroccan authorities, and early in 1972 *Souffles* and *Anfas* were banned. Shortly thereafter, more than 200 Moroccan writers, artists and intellectuals were rounded up. Many were imprisoned, tortured and sentenced to long prison terms. Some went insane as a result of the torture, others died, and still others remain imprisoned to this day.

Laâbi survived, weakened physically but with his imagination on fire, and the outpouring of his works – written during the years of imprisonment and since his release – have had a significant impact in Europe and the Arab world.

Although much of his writing first gained recognition in the original French, Laâbi remains a quintessentially Arab writer concerned, throughout his work, with the heritage, history and aspirations both of his native Morocco, and of the Arab nation – that constellation of widely diverse lands linked by their shared language. His personal history has made him a true bilingual, and he recognises that his complete expression can come only from sounding – and in a sense fusing – his two linguistic registers. His answer to the dilemma of the bilingual author is to embrace both languages: "Given the moment of history in which I am living, I personally lay claim to Arabic as much as to French. I communicate in the one what I cannot communicate in the other. When I add them together, I express myself fully. I no longer have a sense of linguistic exile or conflict. I simply have to do twice the work of a monolingual writer."

He continues to move between Arabic and French – through translations of his own work into Arabic, through original writing in Arabic, and through his superb translations into French of the works of a number of major contemporary Arab authors, including the Palestinian poet Mahmoud Darwish, the Moroccan poet Abdallah Zrika, the Iraqi poet Abdelwahab Al Bayati and the Syrian novelist Hanna Minna.

The pervasiveness of barbarism is a major theme in a body of work which traces official cruelty from the author's native Morocco to Israel and the Occupied Territories, from Chile to the Gulag Archipelago. His poetry is haunted by torturers and prisoners, by screams and hunger strikes, and many of the titles in French bear witness to his preoccupation with – and resistance to – the growing international sickness of state-supported inhumanity: *L'écorché vif (Skinned Alive), Le règne de barbarie (The Reign of Barbarism), Sous le bâillon, le poème (The Poem Beneath the Gag), La brûlure des interrogations (The Burn of Interrogations), L'histoire des sept crucifiés de l'espoir (The Story of Seven Crucifixions of Hope),* and the original French title of the present text, *Le chemin des ordalies (The Path of Ordeals).*

Yet Laâbi's work is never simply a cry of rage, nor does he focus primarily on the individual ordeal. When translating the present work from French to Arabic, he chose not to retain the original title, but instead to call it *Majnoun al amal (The Fool of Hope).* Moreover, all his work reaches for a balance between witnessing the barbarism across the planet and rediscovering the voice of hope and justice. Poetry, the undeniable force of imagination, leads to the rebirth of hope, and Laâbi's poetic voice consistently raises a song of possibilities above the dirge of cruelty. His only weapon against the armed men, the instruments of torture, and the citadels of incarceration, has always been a pure language that wells up from deep within; and what propels that language, what gives that imagination its full power, is that it emerges from a man possessed by hope – not a fragile, fairy-tale hope, but a vibrant, soaring hope, a hope more real than the barbarism that would devour it.

Laâbi has long insisted on the social function of poetry, its power to revitalize and transform, and to record and convey history, uncorrupted. In this sense his work can be compared to that of the Polish poet Czeslaw Milosz, whose poem "Destiny" echoes Laâbi's own poetic creed:

What is poetry which does not save
Nations or people?
A connivance with official lies,
A song of drunkards whose throats
    will be cut in a moment,
Readings for sophomore girls.

Rue du Retour is of a piece with Laâbi's poetry; in it he does more than chronicle the experience of savage torture and isolation and imprisonment – he probes the deepest recesses of the tortured, imprisoned self, and gives expression to one of the most compelling, urgent voices in modern times to be raised against state barbarism.

In an interview published in 1985 he defined his central concerns in the work:

"As for the approach I took to my experience of prison, I could have drifted into an almost canonized genre: the series of portraits, the humiliations, the physical and psychological suffering, etc. But what concerned me most – beyond these realities, which I have not evaded – was to account for the way in which a man could 'function' in such conditions: the extraordinary expansion of his inner world, his haunting encounter with himself, the atrophy of some of his faculties combined with the heightening of others, his waking and sleeping dreams, and, perhaps more than all of that, the way in which a man, cast into a situation he had not foreseen or even imagined, gradually manages to infuse it with his own values, to humanise it, to lend it a certain rationality – in short, to dash all prison's bars, even the supposedly unbreakable system itself, by summoning up his human ingenuity, his capacities to adapt, to give of himself, to love . . ."

Rue du Retour charts Laâbi's itinerary from the chaos of oppression to the cosmos of hope. One of the essential revelations to spring from this prison experience is the sustaining, expanding quality of love, and the magical ways in which people can become bonded to one another. His profound relationships with his wife Jocelyne (whom he addresses in the text as "Awdah", Arabic for "return"), his children, his fellow prisoners and prisoners of conscience everywhere, become an indispensable element in his strategy to survive, and a recurring theme throughout his work.

It is to be hoped that the translation of this moving, luminous book will be but the first note sounded in the English-speaking world by the voice of a poet who deserves our attention, our respect and our gratitude.

Victor Reinking, University of
Washington at Seattle, 1989

Rue du Retour

Finally the exile ceases
the hands with their long burns of waiting
happiness like open veins
and the round which never stops unwinding itself
to the furthermost reaches of the dream
There
without embellishments
without addition of comfort
my eyes encrusted in each wall
each bench spattered
by the blood of a scream
there
site of the ordeal
Marked by this twilight
which lashes me
and lashes me yet

1.

Free. Old salt of the prison seas. You are free. Three pairs of eyes survey you, looks awash with envy, stupidity, fear and respect. A servile confusion. As usual, obedience is tempered with panic. But there is no appeal against orders. Nor any point in trying to understand them. Even if it means saying black is white and vice versa. No appeal. Carry them out, just carry them out.

In this small office redolent of the comforts of an oasis in the heart of the prison-desert.

Here where you have often come to ask for or to protest about your letters, parcels gone missing, about a scarf which contravened regulations because it might have been used in some cunningly worked-out suicide, about a visit banned, though paradoxically it had been allowed the week before, about a spiral-backed notebook judged to be a threat to the security of the Institution . . . About all the petty things which allow Authority to establish itself, deadly and complete, under the guise of order.

"Give us your address on the outside."
"3 rue du Retour."
"That's where you're planning to go?"
"Of course."

Awdah. In spite of all the powers of our imaginings, we never thought of this moment, this precise day, plucked so arbitrarily out of the length of the sentence.

Now look at me. My heart is not beating wildly. There is no catch in my throat. A strange indifference. I haven't even got the kind of stomach cramp I get when I want to write a poem and when I spend hours whirling round my cellular promontory.

"Now go and get your things together."

It's the highest-ranking of the three who gives you this final order.

You don't reply. Your head is empty. You feel slightly disgusted. It's the same feeling as you get when a hand remains absent-mindedly on your shoulder. You want to get rid of it, but you can't be too obvious about it because you might cause offence.

The eyes still trained on you. You think you can see something resembling embarrassment in them. Could they be excusing themselves for having carried out an order which might just as well have been for your execution? Are they asking you not to turn around if you pass them in the common streets?

But perhaps these eyes express nothing. Just some meaningless blinkings from the administrative machine. That's all.

Awdah. It's you who first shatters my indifference. Will you believe me?

I left the governor's office and went back to the wing to get my things together. In order to do that, I had to cross the large, inside yard where there is a fountain, the stone seats and the large watchful palm tree which is right in the middle and which stands up like an acrobat on stilts, pushing all its fronds to the top. This is the palm whose top I could see during my walks and which I contemplated at the end of every afternoon before returning to my cell for my solitary evening.

Will you believe me?

All of a sudden everything was in turmoil. I was walking towards the palm or rather it was coming towards me. And suddenly it caught fire. There was only a cloud of smoke where it had been. And through this smoke you appeared to me. You were being reborn from the ashes of the tree and of woman. You were taking shape, swathed in a purple shroud which you were pulling and tearing at with the same kind of intensity which used to transfigure you when we merged androgynously, one body, panting with the delirium of life. And the shroud was being carried off in a sheet of flame, your arms were opening . . .

"Let's go. Get a move on please!"

That was the voice of the warder who was taking you back. You were forced to tear yourself away from this apparition. Time was pressing on.

Time. Don't let it be lost on you, the profoundness of the transformation. It's your first skin to lose, old camel from the deserts of empty time. Listen, listen hard to the chimes of the clock which has just struck from the very depths of the night and whose vibrations will soon echo round your head.

Time. Later you will look it up in your old dictionaries and your new physics books. You will read again the philosophers who closely observed its passing, while stretched out on the banks of rivers, their ears attuned to the pulse of the sky.

But for now don't try to analyse it. Enjoy it. This moment. This fraction of eternity, which by itself is shattering the apparently immutable, snapping the patina of silence.

Awdah. How to understand the portent of that vision? For some hours yet I would still have time to wonder. To rack my brains over which ancient myth it was had flashed before me, or to sift more prosaic scenes: remembered bits of reading, movie clichés, my own crazy inventions from slack moments when I became too much the poet even for my own liking.

Death — rebirth. To leave the citadel. The friends who must stay behind for months, for years, perhaps for a life like the one that has just ended for me. And you, my next horizon. Both of us experiencing the pain of rediscovery.

"Congratulations. Take care of yourself. Don't forget anything."
"Thank you, comrades, thank you."
"No, above all, don't forget."

Powerful embraces. Terrible embraces. Our hands clasped together in spite of all their wounds valued highly as the price of honour, in spite of the disillusions of everyday life, the lack of dignity in enforced intimacy. Our hands clasped together because not all our dreams have been destroyed. Because men will always remain, whatever the calamity. Because we sang together as one, though some struck up only half-heartedly. Because of that cloak which used to descend each night over our heads, reducing us to a pulp of bruises and of flesh exuding the sweat of exile, and because of that sun which we shared each morning to enliven our banal greetings. Not to mention the shared bread of suffering and of hope.

Terrible embraces. What can we exchange at the moment of parting? You, already marked, charged with the wild magnetism of freedom, breathing your Promise into the bellies and faces of those you clasp against you. They, releasing into you their limitless warmth and the dreadful burden of their bitterness and exhaustion.

The noise dies away. The final notes of the song. Laughter. Hidden by the screen of padlocked doors. This time it's behind you.

"Let's go. Let's get a move on please."

The warder helps you to carry your things. Cardboard boxes into which you have thrown together a few clothes, a few books, letters from your wife and your friends, school exercise books crammed full of notes and poems. That's all. There won't be any presents for your children as souvenirs of your long journey. You have forgotten how to use money.

No, you cannot take back anything substantial. You feel as light as the winged angel in religious stories. Only your head feels a bit heavy on your weak shoulders. In fact, what were you bringing back?

"Wait here a minute." The warder goes off.

Once again, the large inside yard. The fountain's

5

murmuring as usual. The palm is back in place. The wind rustles through its rough fronds. It's the same tree you gazed at every day as the yard was emptying, and you managed to evade the warder's eye so that you could stay behind for a few minutes, just for that encounter. Palm versus prisoner, palm/prisoner. Every possible variation. Because there was a sort of conspiracy to commune. Each held a mirror up to the other. Silent secrets reflecting silent secrets. The sap circulated from one body to the other. The wind stirred both your manes. Yes, in certain circumstances a tree can grow a man.

"Follow me. We're going to the depository."

The warder pushes the big gates which lead to the prison wings. We rush down the staircase. Wide, stately steps fit for a church or an Aztec temple. A glimpse of the central block. A bogus womb which gently sucks you in. Right hand side: the death cells and solitary confinement. Left hand side: the workshops and another solitary block. Out of sight at the end: the main wing made up of several floors housing those sentenced under common law.

Your feet slip on the shiny floor and your head spins with images provoking conditional reflexes. So many toings and froings across this block. This was your outside world whenever you left the wing to go to the administration offices or for the highlight of the week, the visit which you had baptised in your quasi-esoteric language, "the rite of union". Crossing this block. It used to seem to you like a journey which teetered on the edge of a fragmentary freedom. It was here that you laughed, cried with happiness or with the homesickness you usually suppressed, heard the fresh news you shared with your fellow travellers.

"Later on, we can make this into a university." How often you voiced this utopian commonplace.

"Have you any property here?"
"I can't really remember."
"What's your number?"
"18 611."
"Yes, there's something belonging to you."

Some numbered sacks have already been pulled out. You turn aside to enter the depository. A set of small rooms with rows of rails along the walls from top to bottom. No smell of naphthalene or chloroform. But the sensation of being in a cave. In shadow. In a vice of silence.

Through the rows of rails, the sacks can be seen, leaning against one another. Like small corpses collapsing under the weight of the law of time without value. Baby mammoths transfixed by a social apocalypse.

"Here are your things. Sign here."
You open the sack with your name on it. You hesitate. You try hard to remember the moment when you took off civilian clothes to put on the prison uniform. Before you can pursue your silent conjectures you have pulled out the green velvet suit. You are spreading it out and touching it in a daze. It's all crumpled and creased. It looks as though it has shrunk. You are invaded by the spirit of Beirut. Yes, you were wearing this very outfit when you went to Beirut to engage with the diaspora of Arab poets. It was there you launched an attack on the Egyptian diva to the horror of the fanatics of all

sides. But the young people in the hall had applauded you. You had got rid of a thorn in the flesh. Or had you in fact simply displaced it?

You speak about young people as if at a distance, old camel from the deserts of empty time. How old are you, then?

"Let's go. Let's get a move on please."

Across the central block again. This time a single image forms itself on you, it overwhelms you. It disorients you. You stop to try to get your balance. When was that? No, you can't forget. Remember. "Our people cannot forget." That other thorn, "planted in the heart of memory". Now you remember. It was the night of 26 August 1974. You were in the solitary confinement block. Late at night. You were reading a book by Gorky or about Gorky. You had stopped to think about his remark, "It's impossible to write great novels when you are afraid." The lights suddenly went out. From other cells came shouts of protest. You had gone to the judas hole and called for a warder. No warder. You had begun to pound on the door just as the others were doing in all the cells. Then, exhausted, you gave up. But what surprised you was that at the same moment the noise also stopped in the other cells. Everyone had given up at the same time. A synchronic silence. It was the same phenomenon as sometimes occurred when prisoners and visitors all stopped talking at the same time. And it created the same unease. For a few seconds no one would dare to start talking again for fear of exposing themselves.

The warder did not come. The electrician, who used to come quite quickly when there was a blackout, did not come either. So there was something unusual going on. A long silence. From time to time a comrade gave a derisory whistle. But the silence prevailed. The whole wing was listening.

Echoes arose from the central block: gates being opened and closed. Shouted orders. Metallic steps. Mixed cries and laughter.

An escape attempt? A new group of prisoners being brought in? Or others being transferred? It was pointless to pursue these speculations. This lasted for at least an hour. The light came back on. The book by or about Gorky was there, open on your stomach. You picked it up again. But you were hardly reading. You were thinking about Siberia under the Tsars and modern gulags. Your eyes were wandering round the walls of your cell, panning across objects like Fellini's camera.

"Poor Gorky!" you finally said, without knowing why. And you fell asleep. Next day you, along with everyone else, heard about the release of some prisoners and the execution of seven others.

You did not hear the shots. You were too deeply asleep. You dreamed you were in a gulag. You finally ended up disembarking somewhere along the shores of the Amazon amongst a tribe going through a transitional stage of development from matriarchy to some other condition. And you were putting yourself forward for election.

Come on old camel, you have already told that story.

"Form into groups of ten!"
You were in the first group. Amongst those about to undergo the baptism of freedom there were several of your friends. A transmigration. A flight from

9

one body to another. To take root behind veiled eyes where each savoured his own sensations. The kind of persistent images which overwhelm sight. That's what makes knowing people so complicated. Each person, whatever his social and economic conditions, preserves within himself an irreducible kernel which eludes every technique for analysing groups. For example, what's going through the mind of this patriarch who has spent twenty years in jail and who in a few moments will inevitably find himself on the outside? You try to catch his eye in the poor light of the yard. You look at each other. But he does not see you. His eyes mimic vacancy. What can freedom mean after so many years, so many upheavals? One day you had discussed, or perhaps heard someone else discussing with him, the state of the country, international politics, the town he used to live in. From what he said one thing was obvious. He was still living in 1960. Casablanca had not changed. Its streets still carried the names of French colonial officers and administrators. Egypt was still living through the euphoria of Nasser's rule. Palestine was on the verge of liberation. Nkrumah and Sukarno were the hope of the Third World. Russia was helping the Arabs.

And this old peasant from the Middle Atlas. What can he be thinking about? You know him well because you have often listened to him telling stories about the Resistance, the Army of Liberation. A master story-teller, one of a dying breed. You did not take his tales too literally. His memory and his pride embellished them. In a world which lacks real values you realise that men will conjure up their own to live by, to conform or to resist. You can understand, it's a kind of winnowing process. In the end this man who has conceived of his whole life as a pattern of refusal and rebellion has finished up back at the same spot, but now he has seen his family scattered and has lost the land he loved so passionately.

He squats down and covers his eyes. He looks as though he is weeping about his sudden freedom. And his improbable misery infects you.

"Line up for the search."

The warder stands in front of you. He is young. An old acquaintance. He has the kind of smile which makes you automatically raise your arms. It's your last concession to old habits. He runs his hands through your hair, fingers the lapels of your jacket, feels your shoulder, pats your armpits a few times as if he were tickling you. He runs his hands down your sides, round your waist, and then down your thighs, between your legs and back up to feel your testicles.

Arms above your head, but head in the stars, you are in this yard for the last time. The mane of the palm is spread by the gentle breeze of the citadel.

Awdah. Am I really that indifferent? I'm ignoring the warder. It's the palm which fascinates me. It's beautiful isn't it? I would like to understand why, here and now. Am I in the process of sowing the first seeds of nostalgia? Have I just said nostalgia? Why did I say that? The tree stands for something. Is it simply a memento of that secret communion nurtured throughout my sentence by moments of self-rediscovery I felt at the sight of those free-waving fronds? Or has it a deeper meaning? The life

11

I leave behind but from which I can no longer remain detached. To be free again after all these years, with an ordinary liberty which is clearly both precarious and partial but which, when all is said and done, is liberty nevertheless, where one humbly partakes of the general run of misery, garbled communications, powerlessness brandished in one's face, and the assassination of any force for life that represents a threat.

But that other freedom. That of the tree. Of thought. Undefiled. Waking and movement and work, a monastic life purified every day in the cleansing waters of poverty, simplicity and the satisfaction of basic needs. And our union, too. Its inexhaustible power. The ordeal itself. Yes, I love and I shall love.

How mad I have become with thinking about things like this, with such a lack of detachment. It's childish. A boy poet.

Awdah. I'm sorry. I'm revealing myself as I truly am. I don't spin fantasies to enhance my correctness or my "normality". My life is not for sale.

"What are those papers?"

"Sorry?"

"More poems! Well, when you publish them, send me a copy of the book, will you?"

"No, they're personal letters."

The warder does not pursue it. He's rooting deeper in the cardboard boxes. He turns over the photos. He's looking at a writing pad which has been stiffened and covered with a plastic wrapper.

"What's this?"

"My desk."

He laughs. He goes through the books with a fine tooth comb.

"If you're looking for money, there isn't any."

"O.K. Good luck. Next!"

There are now ten of you in front of the prison gates. Take a good look at this monument, old camel from the deserts of empty time. And have a mind for your skin, you'll be shedding it in a minute. But above all, have a look at this monument. You have never really been up to describing it. You lack architectural and mathematical talent. You have never had a strong sense of size or of measurements. You are staggered by this masterpiece of prison design: panopticon, doors festooned with hinges, locks, bolts and keys, apparently for the use of a race of giants. But you elude the feeling, your mind half-engaged with the palm, of which you can now only see the top, half with the group of men pressed against one another in order to share their thoughts or bolster their courage. You cast your eye over them. Why them? Why you, and not others? You have a strong intuition of some powerful caprice governed by necessity. Local political habits being what they are. But you give up trying to figure it out. Your indifference is a kind of defence mechanism against an unpleasant tendency to egoism. In any case, you realise clearly that this is no gift that someone has given you.

You look at your companions: diverse ages, diverse social groups. A representative sample of your fellow countrymen are now being returned to them. On the outside, life has not ground to a halt, however much one thinks it ought to have. Life either ignores or cares very little about those who have been absent. It

13

recreates men and matter ceaselessly. It pursues its hieratic purpose which you can never really get to the bottom of. You can barely grasp the meaning of the ripples which ruffle its surface. This land, just two steps away. How will you rediscover it with your own eyes, ears, hands? Not to mention the wider world which has been shaken by so many earthquakes which have annihilated some of your finest dreams of justice.

This nation-people which flows in great surges behind the heavy metal doors and to whom you have nothing to offer but your healed wounds, the willing sacrifice of the best years of your youth, your heart intact but scarred by the red hot iron of your unwavering anger.

All these ten, and those who follow them, are being reborn into a death which will one day eventually throw in its hand and give way to a universal coming-to-life.

Trak Trak! The gigantic warder pulls at one of the gates which sticks for a minute and then moves through its steel semi-circle.

"Off you go!"

Farewell, my brother palm.

Thank you, comrades, thank you. No, above all there will be no forgetting.

You cross the threshold. The gate closes swiftly with a deafening clash. Just like a gong being struck. It's as if some fire-raising tyrant had decided to set off the alarm, another practical joke played on his courtiers.

Boom!

A kind of shock-wave hits you in the stomach,

spreading out to the rough edges of your body. You are seized by the kind of feeling a space traveller must get as his spaceship leaves the earth's field of gravity. This, at least in the old science-fiction films, used to be shown as the moment of greatest physical strain.

Off you go then, old camel from the deserts of empty time. Give thanks to the starry night for your deliverance.

You shake yourself mentally to throw off the vibration. And you move forward. One step, then two.

You will have to learn to walk again. One step, then another, always forward, in a straight line. It will no longer be that round, that circling around which inevitably ground to a halt at some point during your journey. This circling which will certainly have left its mark on your senses, forming your thoughts into concentric circles with all the consequences implied by that. But for the moment you are unable to assess whether that is a good or bad thing, nor to appreciate its richness or sterility. It just reminds you – by a simple association of ideas – of the cyclical law of Ibn Khaldoun and the narrative structure of *A Thousand and One Nights* (glimpses of your bookish culture).

One step, then the other, you're going neither forward nor backward. What is certain is that you are approaching the sky. You had instinctively lifted up your eyes. And the sky fits into place over your head. The whole sky. Not just a bit which disappears or is fragmented by one of the many tricks of prison architecture.

Astronomy is not your strong point. But at this moment you are grateful for your ignorance. For you do not need to read the sky's map. You only want to soak yourself in this cold rain from the stars and feel on your face the drizzling light they are sending towards you, to open your eyes and receive this mighty embrace.

This then is your first upheaval.

And the night galloping past. A huge gathering of constellations, an uncontrollable breeze which plays in every corner of the warm darkness, the lights of the town spread out like a mushroom, richly appealing, the spongy earth springy beneath your feet. All this, and your heart is expanding to contain this anonymous offering.

Free!

Now do you understand?

"Welcome. Greetings!"

Hands held out. Embraces. Faces unknown or known on rare visits, through bars. A small group who had succeeded in penetrating the mystery of the gods and who were there for the welcome. Mostly lawyers.

It is clear from certain gestures that they have not come for you. You are not a part of their family, the Tribe of Great Realists for the Good of the People. An eternal dissident. In the past you had dared to raise your hand against their monolithic temple which claimed to represent the people and their aspirations. Despite the passing years you had never admitted your blindness. You had not finished up by conceding the realities, the correctness of your elders, their justifications which you insultingly and hot-headedly associated with compromise. You had not been invaded by that easy wisdom which dictates

16

embracing the hand one cannot cut off. You had nothing to offer to the ideological dullards, to social segmentation, to the theory of elites, to groundswells of opinion, to the stages theory, to specificities. A poet. As such, they could appreciate you without understanding, because, after all, it was better to have "the intellectuals" with them than against them; and so, according to how docile you were, flatter you, even anoint you the prince of poets of this sunny land, believing thus you would be muzzled. The deadly pride of the artist. Now please, no politics, no right of conscience, for lyricism is not fashionable, because one cannot draw up battle plans with good feelings alone, for loyalty is not a collar kept only for dogs.

But perhaps you're imagining all this, old camel from the deserts of empty time. Who told you that exclusiveness and mistrust always prevail? Don't forget that another permanent facet of local custom consists of smoothing, clipping the wings of contradictions, strengthening the family spirit and a kind of sickly-sweet brotherhood (not that which you have always called for, the strong-sweetness of brotherhood, the sharing of your sun), the comforting snore of unanimity. And you should also take into account that superstitious mediocrity which puts up with anything from the sacred, extravagant artist, provided he toes the line. Let him be produced for big occasions, parades, shows of unity and strength, to capture the imagination of the helpless crowds.

You have a value now. Old salt of the prison seas. You are like a virgin who has achieved goodness by long suffering. Your exile, your pains, your white hair and the size of your waistline which you have managed to keep in spite of the weight of the passing years – all that creates an irresistible charm, the honeypot to which will be drawn many of these players-of-the-politicians'-game, many a Don Quixote inspired by the romance of your return.

Take care. Now at last you might make a few feathers fly.

"I'll go with you."

The man with whom you fall into step is dark, thick-set, affable.

You know him slightly as someone who could keep his distance from the Tribe of Great Realists for the Good of the People. But, after all these years, you're not prepared to swear to anything. This is, in any case, one of the first principles of the conduct which now imposes itself on you and becomes part of your ethics-in-formation. Also perhaps just an acquired deformation – you are always on the look-out, with a feeling of always being followed, totally alert, watching for the smallest gesture, the least word which might be a prey for the eyes and ears in the walls. Being under close observation creates bizarre reactions. One eventually begins to spy upon oneself, one interiorises suspicion. Watchfulness as a psychic phenomenon is nothing other than this internal splitting.

"How's your health?"

"O.K. But good morale is more important."

The man drives carefully and confidently. He is like someone carrying a fragile cargo who wishes to avoid any jolt.

The car is an island of comfort. The dashboard with

18

its posy of instruments bears witness to the cost of the machine. The engine is like a bee which buzzes under glass.

You settle back in your seat and stretch out your legs.

The car goes down the slope alongside the cemetery. In both Casablanca and Rabat the prison adjoins a cemetery. In fact in Casablanca the prison is known as Ghbila (*cemetery* in prison slang). A coincidence/ local characteristic, or a "universal" phenomenon? The secret of this mystery is to be found in another country. The modern prison system was a creation of the old Protectorate. Besides, you have often been told, the system is controlled by the Law of 1915, amended and supplemented by the Law of 1935. The post-colonial *ijtihad* stopped short at the prison walls. It did not touch them. To be sure there were more urgent matters than the reorganization of the kingdom of the dead and the half-dead.

"When did the Administration tell you?"
"Towards the end of the afternoon."
"Does your wife know?"
"I don't think so."

The car passes the cemetery, turns left and heads in the direction of the town.

Death. A new object of contemplation. Before, you used to regard it more as a subject for a student dissertation, making a change from themes like the ambiguity of scientific progress or a commentary on a bit of Hegelian bravura. An abstract idea whose outcome could be set out in manuals, or a hobby-horse which seemed slightly foolish.

As with so many other things, you discovered its

19

reality most unexpectedly. As with so many other things, you had no time for investigations. No research, comparison, synthesis, experiment. No question of insight vs practice or a combination of the two. It lay in wait for you, like an electric shock. And it burned its mark on your flesh, and then you knew, not just another event in your memory-bank but a thorn, a blade, no matter the instrument or the image. You were marked. There it was.

So death was experienced through successive illuminations, through chance, through instinctive panic.

Remind yourself of that storeroom you ended up falling into after the preliminary, civilised oral interrogations.

The Guardian of Prosperity charged with this task had already warned you. He had in fact got *carte blanche*. You would not be able to leave alive if you did not say what had to be said. Furthermore, he had tried the usual methods, struck the right notes of appeal. Your social position. Your status as an intellectual. That you were not, after all, one of the masterminds and those others who were the masterminds were the ones who should suffer. That no one wished you any harm. That it was not you personally who was wanted. That what really interested them was the useful information you could let them have. After that you would be free, released, cleared.

You now recall his head. A playboy with a beauty spot on his cheek that gave him a foppish air. But with the voice of a wild animal and the look of his profession. Yes, you were not deceived, you have never been deceived about that kind of look. The

Guardians of Prosperity have in their eyes a special sign, a gleam of hatred for life, for anything out of the ordinary, for intelligence – however it may manifest itself – a gleam that oozes death. This glassy look is like shears rusted by hatred.

"You must be hungry."

"Yes, a bit."

"Then we'll first go to my place to have something to eat."

The storeroom recomposes itself before your eyes as the car goes down one of the main roads of the town. Yellow lights from the lamps spread out as the car slows, illuminating the interior in fits and starts. You see a radio-cassette player.

"A little music?"

"Yes. Thank you."

The man puts a cassette into the player. Presses a button. A moment of uncertainty. The music flares. Fortunately it's not a song. It's a classical piece. Mozart perhaps. The sound does not flow into your ears. It's not your sense of hearing which comes into play or is called upon. Rather you feel yourself enveloped, then anointed, massaged along the whole length of your body by this music. Your joints relax, your muscles unclench, a kind of lascivity takes you over while the notes run through your veins, dissolving into the sap which irrigates your body.

Awdah. They came to get me that morning. The day of the Feast of the Sacrifice. Later, we would learn this was not a coincidence. A year later, on the same day, other men were to know something worse. Their blood ran at the same time as that of the millions of sheep whose throats were cut in all four corners of the country, and further afield, throughout the whole land of Islam, as a remembrance of and lesson about the sacrifice of Abraham. The year after, it was the same. Abraham had not heard the voice of the Angel. He had been turned into a blind executioner. Ismail was lying dead in his own blood and there was no one to intercede. Abraham opened his eyes when it was too late. He abandoned prophecy. From that moment onwards his rule was known only for its scorched earth policy. No one dared any longer open the Book to compare the letter with the spirit.

These were the years of the great fear when one saw towns laid out on grids; the kidnapped in chains. Villages burnt with their harvests, pregnant women thrown into dungeons to be tortured, giving birth in the darkness amidst the cries of the tormented. Old men chained to adolescents, sharing their sighs, their doubt and the vermin which rampaged from body to body, carrying fever, the unbearable anguish of still being alive. Disused hangars, dirty cellars where lay hundreds of "packets of human bruises" to whom it was forbidden to speak, coughing, sighing, tossing on the one thin blanket which served them as a bed. Forbidden to sit down or to call the warder in too high or too low a voice. Forbidden to lift the blindfold, to take off the manacles even while eating the pathetic ration or when going to the toilet. One had to remain all the time lying on one's

22

back, the hands clearly visible above the blanket, and to wait. And when someone was called to go to be questioned it seemed, paradoxically, like a deliverance. To get up, to walk, go down the corridors, to sit on a chair, to speak to someone even if it was the person who ordered you to be taken down to the cellar in order to speed up the confession by using the appropriate methods.

Awdah. How to speak human suffering. The ordinary and so appalling suffering. I say ordinary for it's only here that men can be reduced to their most basic expressions: the cry from the guts which gradually declines into the final death rattle, the instinct to live in spite of all the deformities which reduce life to the kind of voiceless motions mouthed by fish as they foolishly remain still in a tank or at the bottom of the fisherman's basket, the brain which atrophies to the size of a nut as the electric current scrambles ideas, empties the marrow from the bones, reduces the digestive tract to a flabby and bleeding ball. I am talking about this in the most general terms. I am avoiding the temptation to make comparisons. Whether it is more or less inhuman to have one's eyes pierced, to see one's fingers or one's hands chopped off, to have a bucket over the head upon which someone hammers until one becomes deranged, the parrot's perch or drowning, to be hung by the feet or crucified, to be raped oneself or to see one's beloved raped, the blackmail of psychiatry or the sophistication of soundproof cells for murder-by-suicide. Here or in "fraternal" countries, Chile or Israel, West Germany or the countries of the gulag.

23

The particular takes us to the universal and vice-versa. I wanted to say that Abdellatif Zéroual is the twin brother of Victor Jara.* They lived the same barbarity that infects our earth. They will grow together in the bosom of death-and-resurrection.

"How do you feel?"

"I still can't believe it."

The car was leaving the town now. Lamps began to light up the road. All around the forest stretched away in a solid silence.

You had dreamed of this journey so often. Real dreams. With neither car nor plane. You were in a time when men had only the power of their imagination, when their need to conquer the world's mysteries could cost them their lives. You were inside the skin of Icarus whose dream came true. Your wings were carrying you away from the citadel of exile. You were escaping through the tiny window of your cell. First you were perching on the outside wall. The powerful searchlights of the control tower did not melt the wax of your wings. Then you were moving towards the forest. You met a crowd of peaceful eagles who made room for you, took you on a lap of honour. You followed their migration. And finally the sea appeared, as vast as an unknown galaxy. Boats glimmered there. Whales played peacefully with each other. Then suddenly the eagles were giving you the slip. You remained alone looking at the whales and the sea-mastodons. You flew, flew until

---

* The Chilean singer Victor Jara was tortured and killed in September 1973 after a military coup overthrew the government of Salvador Allende. Abdellatif Zéroual, a Moroccan poet and activist, died under torture in November 1974.

you lost your breath and the sea was infinite. You were beginning to lose height, the sea was rising up in a foaming maelstrom. A real dream. But you also often indulged in day-dreams. A scene rather like the one you were now living through. The return-by-fire. Your head in a maze of questions. Your monster camera-eyes registering the least detail. And the inward eyes peering into the past and the future both immediate and distant.

Look at the forest, the tropical creepers with their prolific foliage, the soft resins, the feet which sink into the carpet of dead leaves. Possible footpaths. The laughter of children which you have forgotten all about.

And the car moving at the speed of hope. Of the wings which push towards or of arms reached out for the loved one. You lower the window. Put your head out. The wind plays through your hair. It blows like a gentle hairdryer as you relax into it. Your nostrils quiver and open. You open your mouth. You breathe through your nose, mouth and hair. The music intoxicates you. And you begin to sing like a boy suffering the martyrdom of first love, forgetting the proprieties and the solemnity of the moment.

You write your name on ancient stones
my beloved
You write my name on the wayside sand.
Your name endures
my beloved
my name is erased.

Fayrouz. Voice of an emerging continent. A miracle of peace.

Then the room again where the playboy inter-rogator finally puts you in the hands of the Bogeymen whom he had endlessly threatened you with through-out the preliminary questioning.

"This son of a bitch must talk!" barks the playboy. Then he disappears leaving behind him the sickly smell of his American cigarette.

Well at least they give a bit of time to look around the place. In the weak light of dawn you can make out two tables and a wooden bench. In one corner of the room there are some baskets overflowing with twine, rags and glass bottles. In another corner there's a heavy duty tyre.

Later you'll get to know these objects. You will learn the exact purpose of each accessory in this decor. You will meditate upon the remarkable ingenuity which is capable of selecting the most innocuous bric-a-brac and turning it into formidable instruments of suffering. You will learn to recognise the techniques and different schools in the art of torture.

Later when peace is restored, you will even be able to entertain one day the idea of a dissertation on Torture through the Ages. An approach teeming with information about political power, civilisations, violence as the midwife of history, the resilience of the human material and a lot of other stuff. But that particular morning you were only able to cast a naïve glance towards these mysterious objects and to recognise their disturbing hostility. Knowledge has nothing to do with the brain. It has something to do with the guts. It hovers between the cramp you have in your stomach and the menacing and peremptory halo which surrounds these objects.

"Take your clothes off."

At first you don't understand this command. No one has ever asked you to do anything like this. Except the doctor. But he used to be more precise. He would ask you to lift your shirt or to lower your trousers a bit. Even your lover has never asked you to do it. It was you who would take the initiative in a gesture of impatient frenzy when the passion between you was reaching its climax, surrender was turning into trance and the infinity of the human body.

"Take everything off. Do you understand? Shoes as well."

It's a black giant who is speaking. One of the three Bogeymen. They had started on the preliminaries. The bench had been moved and placed in the middle of the storeroom. The twine was unravelled, the rags unfolded.

You obey.

Since when had you not obeyed? From circle to circle you reach back to your childhood. You rummage through your memory and paradoxically you don't find anything. Obedience? Unknown. Your father was not one of those paterfamilias who haunt many stories set around the edge of the Mediterranean and the Arab world. The dictator in his room, the indestructible kernel of the family and solid unit around which gravitates all economic activity, the dominant ideology, arranged marriages, divorce by decree, religious rituals and festivals. The trunk of a genealogical tree and the hand of Providence in everything. He was a good-natured, small craftsman who left each day to go to work at six o'clock in the morning and came back at eight in the evening. Except on Fridays. A highly precise machine at work in our own apparently drifting and lethargic society, turning its back on productive work. This small artisan had managed to send all his children to the "French-Muslim" school so that they might learn the language of power of those days and understand the mystery of that power.

No, you do not remember obedience at that level. Therefore you never experienced any revolt against your father, something which perhaps explains why you never had any desire to write one of those edifying autobiographies which were a kind of initiatory test in the literature of the colonised.

You take off your coat, your jacket and your shirt. You remove your shoes and your trousers. You discover obedience at its most fundamental level.

Yes, all the same. There had been something similar. The Koranic school where one had to learn the impenetrable verses of the Book to avoid the *falaqa*; the French-Muslim school where one had to concentrate in silence to avoid the teacher's metal ruler and later taboos of language and behaviour which one had to observe to avoid falling into the power of an omnivorous law. That had been, all the same, a matter of obedience by default, a fitting in with systems distinct from violence.

The black giant draws closer. He has a black rag in his hands. You notice his hands. The nails cut short, the fingers grimy.

Later hands will become fascinating objects to you. You will judge men in terms of their hands. That will become the criterion for judging potential gentleness or bestiality.

The giant has already blindfolded your eyes. You feel someone get hold of you, someone makes you sit on a hard object, the bench. It's definitely the bench.

Hearing gradually replaces sight. For suddenly it's not black around you. You see in your head a greyish cloud, shot through with sudden coloured flames. Then the light weakens, the colours slip away and become a blur.

"You're going to speak now."

This bark reaches you at the same time as a large resounding blow to both ears. The massive hands of the black giant were in action. A painful whistle bore through your ear-drums. Another smack. And another. Simultaneously, a blow to the stomach makes you writhe along the bench and winds you. Your ears become the focus of a mesmerising wail.

"Speak, bastard, speak."

The light returns to your head. Constellations explode, rainbows of illuminated bundles sweep through the cavity of your brain. The pain diminishes as the blows increase. Then suddenly, cold wet blackness, in your brain a heaviness, collapse.

"What do you make of these half-measures?"
"Difficult to explain for the moment."
The car had slowed down to go through a small, sleepy village. A few electricity poles, a few buildings thrown up higgledy-piggledy, stuck together resignedly along the road. The music stops. The driver presses the eject button, puts the cassette back, starts it off again. The sounds gurgle out of the machine, rise up and pour forth in a graceful fountain. Your

hand opens as if to capture the elusive wave. You inhale the music deeply to regain consciousness, get rid of this spasm in the heart which torments you, chase away the feverish image which transfixes you in your seat.

"It's Mozart they're killing!" You spit out this well-used phrase which has been on the tip of your tongue for a while. It's what disgusts you a bit about yourself and a lot more about the prostituted-culture which sticks to your skin. The intellectual ghetto. The conditioning from which no one will ever be able to emerge undamaged. Even you, old camel from the deserts of empty time. You who made a religion of being vigilant and a self-mortification of denial. This is all that emerges from your mind as you struggle against the image of the storeroom which presents itself more powerfully than the music, more powerful than the heady spectacle of the road, that meteor-path of gladness.

Once again the storeroom. Or rather, the feeling of being there, the night of the blindfold. You regain consciousness, you feel there are other people in the room. A cabal of lowered voices.

"He's coming round."

"Don't give him time to breathe."

Then in a loud voice:

"You're playing the comedian, eh, bastard? You think you're Taïeb Saddiqi!" (You're about to burst out laughing at this comparison with the famous local comedian. You automatically touch your beard. The obvious source of the comparison.)

But the Bogeymen have no time to lose. They stretch you out on the bench and rope you firmly along the whole length of your body. They put a rag over your face and begin to pour water over it: you instinctively breathe it in through your mouth and nose. At first you take no notice what the liquid tastes like. What's vital is to regulate your rate of absorption in order to have a few seconds to breathe between each deluge. But you let yourself be outstripped by your torturers. They are used to it, they are. The technique has been used so often that it has become infallible. A moment arrives when the brain becomes disconnected from the rest of the body. It is no longer the command centre, the controller which takes all facts into account and distributes information, articulates the limbs and the organs. It is simply cut off but hanging on to just enough energy to continue functioning for its own sake.

In another part of your body your guts continue to churn automatically. The water becomes undrinkable. As soon as you close your mouth, someone pinches your nose. You have to open it again to gargle with this sour liquid which numbs your larynx. Like fish in the tank or at the bottom of the fisherman's basket. You open and close your mouth spasmodically. You weaken and offer no more resistance. A white and bitter cloud takes over your brain. To die, is that all there is to it?

When you come round for the second time, there is a heavy silence in the storeroom. You hear the call of the muezzin in the distance. Which prayer is that? And this connection with time brings you back to reality. Are you alone? Did you say anything during your icy fish-in-the-tank delirium? What time is it really? Will they come back to carry on and when? You try to lift a leg, an arm. A moment of paralysis or hesitation, then you succeed. So you're not tied up.

The voice of the muezzin is lingering over the last verses of the declaration of faith. It proclaims the unity of the power which reigns in heaven and on earth, orders the Universe and Time. The voice itself has something superhuman in it. It enfolds your suffering, lifts you up and deposits you on the raft which is gliding across the shipwreck of your past.

You see yourself as a child in a mosque, by the side of your father. It's the solemn moment of the Friday prayer. The sermon has ended. And the voice of the muezzin is raised. It bears witness to the acceptance of faith, the acceptance of submission, reiterates the supremacy of One. Your heart beats like that of a small bird which has fallen out of its nest and cannot fly back. You do not understand, do not ask questions. You are only a weak, little boy who dares not lift his eyes to the adults and who communes in the multiple body of the *Ummah*. You feel clean and pure and you take into yourself the joy of the Promise. Your examples are the Angels of Paradise. You believe as fervently as the beating of your small heart, like a fledgling in distress, will let you.

Then the muezzin is silent. The one from your past and the present one. The child vanishes and the adult stretched out comes to his senses, feeling sorry for himself. Tears come to his eyes and are quickly soaked up by the blindfold.

The silence continues in the storeroom. A sudden idea. Why not lift the blindfold and look? You take time to weigh up the consequences and the risks, to reflect on the storm which has in a few hours blown away what you, like others, took to be ordinary freedom.

You finally come down on the side of freedom. You carry out an act of disobedience. The blindfold is lifted, you see only shadow around you. Then slowly objects take shape. You are no longer lying on the bench but on one of the tables. The blackened window pane allows a little of the evening's weak light to filter through. On the ground there is a large puddle of greyish water. Empty bottles, rags thrown in a heap. In the corner with the tyre you see a metal rod leaning against the wall. Your eyes turn towards the door of the storeroom. Some clothes are hanging on a hook. Your eyes pass over them and then come back. Perhaps they're yours. In your jacket pocket there's a packet of cigarettes and a lighter. You don't hesitate any longer. You get up and go towards the door. They are in fact your clothes. You look through the jacket. In one of the pockets you find your cigarettes. You take one. You light it and return to your place. On your makeshift bed, pulling non-stop on your cigarette, you feel a new strength. In your heart the inimitable sensation of freedom and happiness. You have become brave enough to get up again, go to the door, take your coat and put it on. Then you come back and perch on the table. You smoke while trying to keep your mind a blank. To merge with the movement of the life-restoring sap which is once again beginning to irrigate your body, gathering together the severed and broken pieces. The miracle of being alive. To be a man is nothing except the awareness of this miracle. To shield this pulsing which synchronises all men. To refuse to allow it to be throttled. To connect ourselves in this way to the pulse of the world and to the inimitable adventure of unfolding life.

"He's awake, the bastard! He's lifted the blindfold!"

The door opens suddenly. The Bogeymen rush in. Along with them, other Guardians of Prosperity whom you had not seen before. These put their hands across their eyes, probably so that you will not be able to recognise them. Someone puts on the light. The black giant throws himself at you and pulls off the jacket you had put on. Then the hounds are unleashed.

"Cigarette?"

"No thank you, I'm used to my own." You take a cigarette and light it. The car continues on its ordained way. All around, the forest accompanies it in silent trembling.

Awdah. How can I speak about our separation? That early morning in January. Its meaning for us and for all the men, all the women who lived this tearing apart in their flesh. When combat boots broke into the chamber of intimacy, where troubles are murmured so that they may be soothed away by the hand of understanding, where the heroism of countless poor mothers is expressed in humble and resourceful gestures, where caresses are given or received to heal the wounds of work and hunger, where the secret resistance of the soul is revealed, the hidden patrimony that will always elude interrogations, where every sort of wretched-ness can find shelter, so long as basic dignity be preserved.

But see how those in combat boots violate this secret place. They do not even leave their guns outside the door. They trample on that feeling, the whisper, the caress. They trample on the innocent and humble gesture. They destroy the proud order of years, of presumption of innocence and of mutual respect. They do not investigate, they humiliate. They hate writing and books. They cannot stand anything connected with culture, anything which might show up their weaknesses. Goebbels proclaiming, "When I hear the word culture, I reach for my gun." Yet even at that, we can pause, try to understand. Among other things, the ordeal has allowed us to get beyond the shell of words and to put a finger on that which connects them with the forces which make and unmake history, to the great strategies and mystifications which are thrown up like hurdles during the obstacle course of their inevitable use, put a finger on that which eludes men's consciousness and that which is the master-work of that consciousness, but such a master-work that sometimes it becomes a Pandora's box achieving the seeming inevitability of a work of nature. But alas, everything we have learned about power, its class character, the complex connections between superstructure and that which determines it from beginning to end, turns out to be of little use when we want not only to interpret that famous remark by Goebbels, but to retrace the complex path which led to it, starting from the deepest and most distant of human experiences, conscious and unconscious, from the prehistory of great terrors and wonders up to our own insane civilisations, devouring life's essential forces and arms. Hatred, fear of intelligence and of that which is most subversive in it — freedom, or long ago in the most distant past of man, the taboo against genocide, or awe of woman's power as creator of the greatest mystery.

On what planet of the apes do we find ourselves?

Awdah. I wanted to speak to you about the separation. Ours. Your sleep that morning. Lover-sister-mother-child-wife, multiplying, radiating enigma. You were like that when they came to get me. I would have so liked not to have dragged you from that sleep. I would have liked to have got up alone, opened the door to the men in combat boots, anticipated this other enigma which was waiting for me somewhere beyond our private freedom. At that moment, I would have liked this sleep exactly as I described it to last till the end of time.

This is the way I understood things, for what I was also dreaming about, at that moment, was rejoining, after the trials which awaited me, your fertile sleep, your profuse peacefulness. You see, I was ready to die.

"Give him the third degree. Until he's shitting blood. We have to make this son of a bitch talk!"

You had recognised the voice of the playboy. The blindfold had been replaced. You were shaking with cold in the renewed darkness. The pack were circling round you, snapping at you from all sides, panting. You were overwhelmed by blows. You were covering your head and your face with your arms, you were curling up as much as possible so that only your back

36

was exposed to the hail of blows. The pain was not yet great enough to make you cry out. You were fiercely swallowing it down while biting your lips, grinding your teeth, determinedly screwing up your eyelids over your eyes. You were making yourself as small as possible as if that served to limit the scope of pain or caused the Bogeymen to think (a realisation which might moderate their enthusiasms if they could see themselves from the outside), to take account of the unequal distribution of strength being displayed, one part of it grotesquely small and the other grotesquely huge.

"Stop that now. Do what I told you!"

The blows slackened without stopping altogether. You had time to work out in your mind a preposterous line of reasoning. Orders are never carried out exactly as planned by whoever gave them. There is always a gap, a hiatus.

The Bogeymen would work according to the pattern of their mental limitations, the tramlines of their imaginations and their banal hatred. Even when, simultaneously, they both stopped hitting you, you still got a blow from time to time. At the whim of one or the other in a bizarre rhythm.

Then there was silence. A moment of bitter-tasting peace. You were hiccuping slowly and without making any noise. Your body was turning inside your head like an electrified wound.

"Get down!"

The command was accompanied by a kick in the region of the kidneys. You fell to your knees. Another kick. You collapsed onto your stomach, your arms were bent back and tied. Your feet were also tied at the ankles. You hear the noise of something metal being dragged across the ground. It bumps against your head. They pass it between your hands and then your ankles. A minute later you feel yourself being lifted, hung up. You had suddenly realised what was happening. It was the method called "the parrot's perch". First your head fell down. The blood rushed into it. An indescribable pain began to crawl from vertebra to vertebra. It finally invaded the whole of the spinal column.

"When you are willing to speak, lift your finger."

The pain got stronger and stronger. You could not compare it to any other. Your body was like a massive lead weight hanging from your vertebral column and pulling, pulling.

The more time that went by, the more the pain intensified and became anarchic. It confounded all bodily functions. No respite, no help. Like the infinity of earth or the constellations of the night, there was an infinity of pain. You were living through this voyage, this suffocating passage of a repeated death. No respite, no help. The gods of the moment were none other than those wretched Bogeymen. They were stirring up the blaze with blows and wild shouts. An encircling horde of witch-doctors who had no need even for mystifying masks.

Drumbeats rise around the jungle's sacrificial fire. You see the laughing teeth of the canine pack. Like live coals the eyes of the officiating cannibals are relishing the prospect. You can no longer be sure of the place or the time. The storeroom is a forgotten cave at the margins of the collective memory. Drumbeats begin. The pack dances. A song is struck up, projected in an inarticulate language. You cease to struggle and you admit your status as victim. Your isolated flesh, given over to the enemy's triumph. Your strength will now feed the warlike progress of others, of other manhunts. Your body offered in order to establish the power of gods still suffering from growing pains. You are preparing yourself for the sacrifice.

Awdah. What I am going to say is very difficult. You see, when you take the ordeal as a whole and try to find out where it really hurt most, which wounds one must reopen so the recollection will be of future use, when one sloughs off the old skins, all the times when one has found oneself at a crossroads of the unknown, there is a nodal point where we must pause if we want to get to the heart of the matter. Not because it is a determining factor in understanding the significance of the path taken up until then nor in order to work out strategies for the future, but because it takes us to the most intimate quick of human beings, the real workshop of history, because it recreates for us the most secret combat zone, not only Against and With others, but also and above all In ourselves. And believe me, it's the most terrible struggle that any human being in conditions like ours can engage in.

So here we are. We return to that room. Mine or anyone's. My experience here can be an example. My ordeal is a mere drop in the ocean. The aim is not only to lay bare an experience which is dated and signed, here and now. I have other concerns than that of simply giving evidence. I am thinking of all the martyrs of history, past and to come. I want to speak about the heroism and anonymous suffering, everywhere where the challenge was well and truly to safeguard hope, however realistic or utopian this might be.

So here we are. In the storeroom. The man has been hung up for some hours. His tethered hands and feet are now terribly swollen. His head is balanced in the void. The pain which pounds through his body has reached such a pitch that it evades all possibility of understanding or intuition. Bile gurgles in his throat. They communicate to him for the thousandth time the order to speak. He faints. He regains consciousness. He faints again. The blows fall harder than ever. The pack continues its macabre dance.

The space of a new realisation, the man thinks. He is capable of analysis. He is no longer in the situation where he used to refuse this kind of exercise because he considered it a sign of weakness. Two alternatives clarify themselves in his brain. To live/to die. To speak/not to speak. But the dilemma he has set out does not encompass the realities which the words death and life ordinarily convey. In this exceptional state which torments his consciousness, life is seen as the sign of humiliation. To live, that means lifting a finger, letting go of the first words, the first names, crawling across the exposed and viscous ground of obedience, bringing to the eyes of the Bogeymen the gleam of pleasure which is the flickering of the reign of death. To live, that means cutting off the most valuable part of oneself: the dreams and ideas which can only be conceived of in capitals, the trust which is the umbilical cord of brotherhood, the peace of belonging. Living in the same way as the demented mother who approaches her baby in order to smash its skull. Living, the foul death that begins when the pain stops.

To die. Not to speak. The man tries to turn the dilemma around, to recover its human facets. To conquer death by death. To forget, collapse, detach his body, have done with all material connections, kill every individualistic hope. To die, to keep one's word, to reintegrate and annihilate one's body in the immaterial body of the people, in the hieratic course of time, in the wounded song of the word. To live again in this way as a fragile germination in the flux of anonymity.

Awdah. I have spoken to you now of an absolute dilemma. My aim was not to recount how certain other men resolved it, on which side of the shaded line between life and death they found themselves afterwards. All that belongs to a lesser story. Quantifying is irrelevant.

But away from the tables and balance-sheets, profits and losses, what I want to make clear is that we are ruined if we do not take account of this anguish.

"Are you going to talk, yes or no?"

The blows start raining down again. This time vigorous kicks which reach far up the spinal column. One of the Bogeymen puts his foot between your kidneys and pushes with all his might. You can no longer feel your hands and feet. Your enormous head is balanced in the void like a goatskin crammed and boiling with scorpions.

The dilemma skimming your consciousness becomes blurred. Pain has invaded the whole field of awareness. A scream rises. Wild and endless. It seems to come from the next room. You soon realise that it comes from your own guts. But it's a scream in which you cannot recognise your own voice. Or rather, perhaps you once heard this cry uttered from your own throat in one of the nightmares in which you used to see yourself in one of the old houses of your home town. You were stretched out in a room, nailed to a platform. A gigantic steel hand was slowly coming down from the stucco ceiling, remorselessly drawing closer, was on the point of tearing you apart. And your scream had this same bestial tone. It summed up your endless horror of life without understanding. You were at the stage in your life when you openly denied a social order based upon stagnation and complacency. And your great, adolescent anger made you ill. The scream was still rising. It seemed as if it could never cease. You felt that it was taking with it not only some part of your pain, the impurities of your body, its weight of material attachments but also all the impediments which were preventing the lower level of your consciousness from pouring forth and unleashing its animal nature.

Then another incomprehensible image forced itself on you and made a groove in your head and would not let go. Your cry became Biblical. You felt yourself inside the skin of a man of miracles who became suddenly familiar and who found words in the immensity of his helplessness: *Eli Eli lama sabachthani!*

"We're almost there."

Your heart beats as if it would burst. Your eyes are open but you see nothing. You painfully drag back your sight from the night of the blindfold, of the storeroom, of the parrot's perch where you were gasping your irrational prayer.

Centuries pass before your eyes before you open them on the lights of the town. Rabat-Salé or Jerusalem?

The scream dies in your throat as another song by Fayrouz begins to echo in your head:

For you, city of peace,
I pray.

Then a whole poem of yours, you who cannot recite even four of your verses straight off, a whole poem comes back to you. So you reel it off drunkenly like an act of liberation.

2.

Tell.

Tell, old salt of the prison seas, before you are waylaid and sucked into the vortex of prosaic freedom.

Take care.

This burning in your body and your memory. It's something like the Before and the After of those who groped their way from Hiroshima.

Yes, the unsayable, that's your problem, this difficult task you pursued with head and hands from earliest youth without ever resolving the enigma. From where did you get your language and the inspiration which fixed matter and form, transformed it into meaningful shape out of this drifting iceberg with its melting pools where popular memory boils up in an effervescent mixture?

What is the part played by chance and what by necessity?

You go back over the path of your own history in search of that beardless youth who used to read a Dostoevsky novel at a sitting and write sentimental poems about the street-children of Fes, instead of wearing himself out in a shop like so many stunted adolescents of his age, and so following the traditions of his artisan ancestry. The pale face of this adolescent reappears. He gazes at you with the eyes of a wounded animal. You look at him through the many-veiled night of memory. But you cannot stand this scrutiny for long. Instead of your finding some key to the mystery which haunts you, it is he who seeks in your eyes the explanation for his precocious deviations, for his permanent rootlessness. He gazes at you in your status as his successor and then begins abruptly to ask you to give account of yourself, putting you in the pillory of your omniscience. You turn your gaze away from those eyes open upon eternity, which have become glassy like those of a suicide.

You see, wherever you turn, that it is you yourself who will have to supply the answers, dig them out of your own body, at white heat where your flora, your fauna and the cosmogony of your visions are always restless, as they feel they are trapped. No atavisms. You are no Tom Thumb or one of the new managers of literature. No trail of pebbles or store of souvenirs which might serve to retrace the path and to mark its steps. Your life is set out like the course of a mad meteorite enthralled by the limitlessness of space. You have always rushed in, head-first, without stopping to look at yourself in the mirror. Yes, the unsayable, that's your problem.

And you are called to tell and to keep on telling. At bottom you respond to this need in men who imagine themselves still, as in earlier times, gathered together at evening around large fires to keep away the wild animals and conjure away evil. The voice of the storyteller was raised in this night long ago, ancestor of all opiates.

Tell.

Tell, old salt of the prison seas. You did not know it perhaps. But there you were, already in the role of Scheherazade. Try to understand why you have resumed this tragic privilege. She was the greatest storyteller of your traditional culture only because she lived permanently under an oriental Sword of Damocles. "Write or be killed." There's no need to think of this ultimatum as coming from the mouth of some executioner. Transcend the naïvety of the parable, and you will hear the voice of History speaking. It is referring to one of its most brutal laws: all silence is death by default. Every day that passes without being voiced is a branch broken off your tree of life. And to speak more plainly, each lost word is a voice extinguished, a desperate plea that finds no response, a horror submerged in the slough of mere events.

Remember Scheherazade. Though she was only a harem waif. She stopped writing when she had produced an heir for her bloodthirsty consort. And the harem finally swallowed her up, crushed her in the machinery of palace intrigues, refined slavery and edifying historiographies.

Awdah
here we are on the Continent
of toiling hope
this morning is ours
and so is the sun which is growing for us
behind the window
We are alive aren't we
quick quick
take my hand

3.

Your first awakening. You open your eyes on this miracle which will become familiar day by day. This woman close to you who sleeps her peaceful, sphinx-like sleep. She encircles your chest with her arm and exudes her warm calmness. Her breath caresses your neck. The miracle of her heartbeat in your hand. The early morning slips between the slats of the shutters and begins to light up the room. One by one, objects take shape and colour, the harbingers of a previous existence: the overloaded bookcase which extends across almost all of the opposite wall, the carved wooden desk on top of which are heaped up letters and other things, the panel of *moucharabieh* fretwork hung at the foot of the bed, on the left posters of women soldiers, the guitar in its dust-sheet leaning against one wall. Your eyes fly from one object to another, ransacking the room, while your body is motionless. It's as if you were afraid that changing your position, you would destroy this miraculous harmony which waking up has presented to you. As if you were afraid to see the woman of your waking dreams fly off in a puff of smoke. You are like a newborn baby who emerges from the long umbilical night and whose benumbed senses perceive things with a kind of contemplative detachment and who, if he had been able to speak, would probably have said something like: "So this is it, this is the world!" With this difference, however, that you, you are coming to this world bearing a crushing burden of another and that this aphasia of the sight and of all the senses has its origins in an even more fundamental shock.

Awdah. You are here. Speak to me in your sleep and tell me I'm not dreaming my dream like I did throughout those three thousand and some nights every time my head turned itself into a theatre of shadows.

You were there as well and your lips as they came close to mine had the taste of the last cigarette lit – in a pitiful gesture of generosity – for the condemned man before execution. There were so many Himalayas and deserts between us. We had to cross towns, labyrinths and, when we were within a hair's breadth of one another, we were separated again by flaming ditches and bridges which collapsed at the last minute.

Oh yes! I sometimes had happy dreams. We successfully overcame all obstacles and sometimes even the dream would open with a scene showing us in the greatest intimacy. This dream brought us peace and gave us horses with which to escape from the pursuing hordes. But we were never alone. On island or riverbank, a tiny room or the corner of a labyrinth, as soon as we began to feel happiness, a monstrous eye would push itself between ours and force itself upon us. We had the feeling we were stealing a few seconds from eternity. The mocking eye curtailed us. Then the

Himalayas would rear up, the deserts would unfold themselves again, the dream would become a maelstrom and we ended up with the scene of an earthquake as bridges fell beneath the smiling eye of a remorseless sun.

A footstep behind the door. Did someone knock? A feeling of having been here before. That January dawn almost a decade ago hovered in the silence and half-shadow of the room. A menace which has been since then an integral part of your metabolism. You're so used to it you do not even react physically. But you react by shrivelling inside and straining to listen. It's the same reaction as that of a wild animal who senses its lair is surrounded and whose eyes swivel around in its dark den like sentinels.

Your eyes renew their pillaging. The ceiling of this room is no higher than that of your cell. You start to look at the patches of damp to pick out or imagine shapes, outlines, animal silhouettes or geographers' maps. There, a small poodle stands on its hind legs and here, the southern tip of Africa flanked by the island of Madagascar; further off a pattern that resembles a Rorschach test. You are now falling back on one of the many habits you learned in prison. The prisoner and the ceiling of his cell. A silent, secret dialogue which was an integral part of life like the ritual of eating and that of roll-call. Every evening after the door had been closed, you automatically turned to this dialogue, as others might, after work, go and sit on the terrace of a café to look at passers-by. The ceiling was a second ocean for you. But unlike the sky it offered nothing to your view. No clouds in romantic formations, no swallows playing at acrobats or storks spreading their wings like old, toothless angels. The sun never appeared there nor the stars. But it was an ocean all the same. It was you who gave it life. You projected onto it the film of the day, the catalogue of your most pressing memories, the images you constantly reproduced so that time would not obliterate them. And this passive ocean turned out to be the best possible screen for allowing you to imagine as much as you wanted so that you could assure yourself that your mind still had the power to create. And when you returned from this exercise in a much-needed escapism you felt a little stronger, you had already erased the shock of doors brutally slammed in your face. You would look at the ceiling with a last, conspiratorial glance as if to say: "Ceilings are made to be passed through."

Awdah. You are here. While looking at this ceiling, I'm looking for your hopes. I would like to be at the back of your eyes, fix myself there, to be connected to your vital organs and see with your sleepless eyes this ocean of yours across which you passed to unite with me again. How to speak with your eyes, to borrow your voice from those years of Trial and of small trials which it is impossible for me, on my particular shore, to thread together with the capricious prayer beads of words.

Wake up, Awdah, and speak. Of yourself in the torture of the first separation and the turbulence you lived through, of our wonderful children but also of all the other women, mothers, wives, sisters, all part of us.

I used to hear you, my dear ones, so dear, I used to see you on the other side of the bars when the curtain opened and they allowed us the weekly quarter of an hour to talk. You had all the same face, the same voice. The same anxiety and the same happiness. You gave off the same warmth and the same smell of earth and of love. You had the same noble, high forehead which irresistibly invited a fraternal kiss. I even believe that, whatever your age, you had the same small wrinkle beneath your eyes or cheek, the same white thread gleaming in your long hair. And I would see your hands like a cluster of stars spread out on the grills, radiating kindness, closing and opening, tapping angrily on the metal and shaking the barbed wire of separation.

I understood you, my dear ones, so dear, unfolding the history of this country and of the world at large. You were our eyes and our lungs outside. You took from far and wide in order to meet our needs. Week after week strong tides of freedom flowed through the grills, you rolled towards us waves of the open sea and we received its fresh spray from the whole swell of humanity.

Through you we soon came to know the price of bread, of oil and of sugar, of meat and vegetables. So we lived more deeply within the harsh struggle of the dispossessed as they sought the means to survive. We shared our people's hunger, the growing lack of the goods of this world they had created with their own hands and with their great, so great good-will. We followed the flux and reflux of their struggle for work, dignity and land. The wall of silence built around their voice by so many

jokes they

reat and

u we

the

l

eyes than all the other boys she can scarcely find the e. She was perhaps the one en he needed to relieve portance brought on by out parting in any secrecy. Or perhaps hat and had merely ng in front of her which she liked e from far off. kitchens, of ich you had n and the on. From iracy of e. From ov

ich

ologies,

e mother

er life, as they

antee of material

omotion, as the man

body, who would make

could choose the colour of

s, she never knew exactly what

ost a source of irritation.

ie young wife who believed she had found
man of her life, a brilliant student with a great
future or an official with his career before him. A
husband like any other, even if he was a little odd –
with those nightly outings from which he returned,
not drunk like the others, but with angry mutter-
ings against the powers that be. If only she could
return to that life now left behind she would accept
any oddities, if that would bring back a home at
peace, turned right-side-up again.

And this sister who, like all the sisters here,
conceals an ambiguous love for her older brother,

more handsome in he
his age among whom
likeness of her secret lov
in whom he confided wl
himself a little of the self-i
a dangerous destiny, wit
material way from the rule o
she knew nothing at all about
contented herself with repeati
friends words from his speeches
for their own sake.

Yes, my dears, so dear, you con
From those lower depths of musty
faded washing and of non-being to wl
been sentenced by the courts of me
centuries-old tradition of sexual divisi
anonymity and beatings. From the consp
fateful nights. From the reign of brute forc
terror set up as human Reason.

You returned from far off. And no one had sl
you the road after that first dawn, branded wit
red-hot iron in your memory, when the men
combat boots exploded into your fragile nest and
tore out its centre. Your diaspora had begun.

Then there were all the possible and imaginable
ways of waiting. Waiting. You already knew
something about that. The existing order exudes
waiting as the liver secretes bile. To wait, at the
door of the hospital, at the employment offices of
factories, in the corridors of administration, at the
doors of the smallest and the greatest holder of
some power or influence, at the foot of the tomb of
some patron saint, intercessor or healer, each time

making your desperate prayer.

You took therefore the road of stand and wait. First at the doors of the commissariats, then the tribunals, finally the prisons. You were at first astonished to find yourself here. In the past you had looked at these queueing men, women and children with a reproachful surprise, as if they could be blamed for having an unlucky ancestry or descendants. And now here you are too, repeating incessantly that your son-husband-brother has not stolen-raped-killed, that he has not been found in possession of *kif*, that he was not arrested while drunk. "Politics", they told you. "He was mixed up in politics." A burning word that they threw in your face and which set you off in contemplation of another mystery. The image of the son-husband-brother was transformed. It appeared in a new light outside of the circle of relations in which you had been used to seeing his actions, to listen to him or to love him. You remembered some of his ideas which at the time you had only listened to in order to be kind: paradoxical fits of anger against the values and the system such as they were and such as they could not help being. You remembered his denouncing your sufferings and those of others, injustices ordinary and extraordinary. Little by little, these words were beginning to take on a prophetic significance in your eyes. "Politics" was gradually losing its aura of mystery and was becoming a familiar word. Moreover, this word that your ordeal had led you to master was being transformed for you into an instrument that every day helped you to understand ordinary life. The humiliation of waiting, what was that, if not politics? The high cost of living was politics as well, as was the lack of jobs, the cancer of corruption, adolescents and children who can find no place in school and who take to drugs or thieving, your cousin who was sacked from the factory because he went on strike to assert his rights – that's politics. Your nephew from the countryside who was beaten because he dared answer back to the *caïd* and who came to find a refuge in your house – that's politics. Your young niece whom poverty urged into prostitution – that's also politics.

Everything was becoming politics. This word, you had succeeded in penetrating its secret. Politics was nothing more than this daily war between rich and poor, those who wielded the club and struck out with all their strength and those who shielded themselves from the blows, those who worked and those who gave, refused or withheld work, those who were silent and those who spoke, those who, through boredom, ate and drank for hours at a time, and those who hungrily swallowed their pitiful portion.

So my dears, so dear, these are the ideas, and many more, which made their way into your consciousness while you waited at the door of the prisons, your arms holding baskets which you had filled with all the things that you had denied yourselves: woollen sweaters, underclothes and warm socks. *Tajine* made with meat, fruit and all the good things you used only to buy for feast days.

Suddenly your relationship with your son-husband-brother had changed. It was no longer

56

only the cry of blood which made you run and wait. What now joined you to him was an entirely new feeling, the finest feeling that can shine forth in the heart of the humble: pride. Yes, you were proud, because you knew that his ideas and the meaning of his struggle were the germs of a new life that you sensed forming itself and pulsing within you, the promise of new-born happiness, such as you had never known.

Awdah. Wake up. You see, I speak so inadequately of you and the others. I feel like a clumsy usurper in describing the splendid conduct of the women on the other side of the bars. Even so I have only talked about those who made up the majority, for whom silence was a bitter lot and for whom prison was a revelation in every way. I have left out the others, those who from the beginning knew what was going on, for whom there was hardly any mystery or in any case a very small one. The trial had not been for them a walk across an unknown continent, on either side of the bars. Awdah, how can I put words into your mouth? I feel I don't have the right. It's time we gave up calling upon women to speak and then speaking in their place. Awdah. Will you speak?

The town is waking up. Below in the street someone is revving his car engine. Two dogs bark in competition. An early rag-and-bone man shouts up to the apartments. The room is now quite light. On the left on the divan you can pick out the patterns and the colours of *zemour* cushions: chevrons, broken waves, crosses, a disconnected system of signs. On your right, fastened to a panel of the glass door, a poster calling for your release and upon which is printed one of your poems: "It will now soon be four years since they tore me from you, from my comrades, from my people." You take a cigarette and light it, while taking care not to move too much, not to change anything in the harmony of that androgynous body that you share with your companion.

Free. You are free. Old camel from the deserts of empty time. In a few moments you will be able to get out of bed, put on the radio, put it on full blast without being afraid that the officer on duty will surprise you or pick on your cell. You will be able to play like a child with that enormous instrument there on the table, pausing at all the stations: France-Inter, Cologne, Madrid, Moscow, BBC, Voice of America. You will be able to put on one of Jara's cassettes, to call on your wife to wake up so that the first kiss of the day will transport you both on the spot into that sweet-tragic pampas of Indian pipes where Victor greets his brothers with music at day-break. You will go to wash and then you will open the door of the house. Yes, you will be able to do it. Open and close the door with these tiny little keys. Then you will go down to the street. You will go to buy bread and milk, all the morning papers. You will read greedily, while standing in the sun, all the national and international news, cultural pages, economics, sports, and with the same greed you will scan social events, advertisements, notices of births, marriages and deaths. All at once you will take in everything said by the officials, the officious and the opposition. You will feel the same drunkenness, the same dull bloating that you used to feel when you drank down a large glass of milk after a long hunger strike.

Do you remember the crazy ideas you had at times like that? You used to imagine the cells of your body as so many Lilliputians in a cartoon. You saw them torpid, worried and desperate after days and days of fasting. The blood agitated them with the same regularity but brought them nothing to eat. The Lilliputians were settled into this state of hibernation when suddenly the blood would well up and become a flood, carrying along with it lots of good things. Tumultuous, mad agitation of the cells who set about ringing the alarm-bells. Cheers and dancing.

You pull on your cigarette, smiling at your cartoon cells and your counterpart who drinks his large glass of milk after a hunger strike. You see yourself again lying on your mattress in your white-washed concrete cubicle. You were awake there as well and you lit your first cigarette. You do not situate this particular awakening in the parade of days, months or years. In the citadel of exile where you surprise yourself in this gesture, the days and the awakenings are terribly alike. Time is an immense hidden clock which strikes beyond the walls somewhere in the belly of a world whose image and outlines are continually changing.

You smoke and listen to the reborn noise of the awakening prison. Clack, clack of the cells being opened in another wing, the grinding of the trolleys on which the warm water and the clear soup of morning are brought, the drawling voices of the heads of the cell-blocks who are calling the roll. Then just above your head, coming from the pathetically small window which barely allows air through, the voluptuous call of a swallow which must be fighting with some sparrow about the hole where she would build her nest.

You look around to reassure yourself or to make a pretence of making sure that you are really there, that the cell has not changed, not moved, that there has not been an earthquake which might have cracked the walls, opened up a hole leading to the river which you would have swum across to reach the forest opposite. No, miracles only happen in dreams. But then, prisoners' dreams are the most jealously hidden, thus the most to be feared, that there are.

The cell has not changed. Two metres fifty by one metre fifty. You are there like a blood-stained sword in its sheath. The walls are in place, thick and solid, the ceiling is bare and empty, like a deserted battlefield. Last evening's book is lying on the right of a cardboard box turned into a bookcase-cum-night-table. On the left, the striped, dark grey uniform hangs from a hook.

You reassure yourself for the thousandth time that you are there, in prison time and space, you scale this peak in your heart every day as it arises from an everyday doubt, which has become systematic and which unchangingly formulates the same question: am I really HERE? Yes, you are THERE. At the same moment you hear a firm footstep in the corridor, the key is roughly turned in the lock and clack, clack, the warder has already opened the door. In one single movement you get up, fold the blankets and straighten the bed. A day like all the others has started for number 18 611.

You go out into the yard which is still covered in

mist. You do a few exercises even if it is an effort. Then you take a cold shower. After that you return to the cell to make your breakfast. Then you go back to the yard to inspect the small area of earth which is cultivated by collective ingenuity as a miniature flower garden. You remember that you had to battle for years with the Administration to make them agree to your digging up this area of earth in the yard. You spell out to yourself the name of each variety of flower as if you had imposed on yourself a kind of initiatory examination into the secrets of nature: sweet-peas, zinnias, sweet williams, snap-dragons, larkspurs. And over there mint, shoots of tomato and chili plants. You go around the square of earth with the same respectful and wondering awe as that of the pilgrim making the circuit around the Kaâba. And it is really true that this square is for you a temple of grace, an island of sweetness and of fragile majesty in the rugged space of a prison laid out in frigid blocks for the containment of the body, the dream and the sky, a vice well-constructed by masterly hands in order to enclose, tie and then cut off the cause of life. Blessed be the graceful flower in the trackless desert! Blessed be the seed, the sprout and the fertile clod of earth! Blessed be the drop of dew which slips delicately over the petal, slides down the stem before evaporating as it touches the grain of sand! Blessed be the perfume which is released by the pistil and the bee which buzzes on the turning collar of pollen! Blessed be the sun which reveals to the uninitiated eye its rainbow and makes us fall madly in love with our land and makes us fully human!

Before leaving you pick a few bindweed which you

put between the pages of a large book or dictionary. Once they are well pressed you will be able to fasten them to the letters you send to your wife and closest friends.

After this circuit, there will be the walk in the yard.

"Good morning comrade, how are you?"

"The prisoner is as well as may be."

A knowing laugh on both sides.

Why do prisoners laugh more than other men? An open, sincere and complete laughter. A mad laughter. From the throat. Convulsive. No words can really describe the phenomenon. Laughter is a part of the same careful hygiene that leads some to wash themselves twice or even three times a day. As if water and laughter were the most effective detergents for the wounds which leave no mark but which swarm over one's body. As if to acknowledge the bitter sense one has of the stupidity that rules the world and of the idiocy hiding behind the mask of order.

The yard is a square or rectangle that your steps make into a circle. Walking is revolving not revolution. When one walks in a circle there is no need to turn back to have a look at the scenery one has travelled through. This walk is not a progression. It's a circuit where the walker takes the scenery with him and where he has the feeling of circling round himself. The animal that turns the grindstone in a cellar wearing blinkers must know something similar. So to escape the vortex, one lifts up one's eyes. The sky is in place. It's an ocean up there. The clouds race, they hold out mischievous arms, terrifying mouths of extinct dinosaurs, smoky wings that they let fall in a silent heap on their flanks. A plane seems as uncanny as a Martian spaceship and disappears behind the wall leaving behind for a few seconds the multi-coloured trail of its flashing lights. Birds free-fall and when they are about to crash they take off again, cohere, twin in a spiral and then fly away in battalions of small sects or tribes. But you are not so stupid as to feel jealous or sad. You peacefully admire this riot of unselfconscious freedom.

Someone calls a number, then your name. You turn around this time, rather irritated. You have never been able to stand the use of the number, so reminiscent of the mortuary. On the other side of the yard a warder brandishes letters addressed to you with an air of self-importance. You hurry over while your heart starts to beat wildly. You take the letters and get away as fast as possible. Like a cat to whom someone has just given a tasty morsel and who runs off as soon as he has it in his mouth to eat it in peace.

A letter from a woman friend whom you have nick-named "The Angel of our Time". It's a gouache, with a floral motif and two hands open in a fraternal gesture. A few simple but poignant words written in many different colours.

A type-written letter from a brother-poet abroad for whom you have become a cause and who talks to you about the lunacy of his writing, of his tribulations in the jungle of publishing, of the totalitarianism with a human face which is surreptitiously infecting the soul and body of his beloved France and who constantly comes back to you, worries about your health and your morale, of the poetry smouldering away and your smile which strengthens his.

Dear brother, he writes for you
the great tree of dreams which left us dreamers
despite the mutilations of electric saws
still displays its sweeter outlines
on the page
spread out
against the most violent storms
against Moloch
even as it rears up in despair.

On the last envelope you recognise your wife's writing. You open it hungrily and begin to read it as you circle the yard, forgetful of the temple of plants, the prisoner's ocean, forgetful of your number.

"I thought about you today. I took the children for a walk in the forest and watched them play. I looked at the trees, the flowers and the colours with your eyes which have not seen them for a long time. I laid in a supply of colours and sensation for you. Hind running off up to his neck in the gorse and gathering up armfuls, Yacine pushing Qods' bike and Qods laughing. The trees which allowed a small glimmer of narrow light through.

"We came back and we have gorse flowers in every corner of the house . . .

"You know, I was dreaming as I came back. I was imagining those times when you used to drive and I used to press myself against you. It was pleasant and moving to think of that, me against you . . .

"I felt a funny sensation this evening. I'll try to explain it to you. But it's difficult to pin down a fleeting impression. Qods had wanted to listen to records, you know, those children's records that Yacine and Hind often used to listen to. Listening with her I found myself carried into the past to the time when I used to listen with them and with you. Then I had the feeling that my way of life had totally changed, and my sense of time in particular. I can't express it any better. I had the feeling that if you had suddenly appeared amongst us you would not have recognised at all our way of living, moving, speaking. We've all become more nervous, quick, less playful, if I can put it that way. We no longer take time to live . . .

"What else? The day drags on and on. A downpour today. An awful downpour which drenched me. The kind of rain one does not see very often. Everyone ran for shelter in any place they could find, porches, arcades. But I was in too much of a hurry. You should see the result! Coat and scarf still soaked and it's more than eight hours ago! And now, you know, I feel as though I am going to have the 'flu! . . .

"Tomorrow, the visit. I would like to talk and chatter to you for a long time.

"The need to be with you, to be there and to wander and say whatever comes into my head, whatever it is. Not to care. Be there, live a little, feel and love passionately. Be there with you, with you all, feel the spirit of comradeship which is the most important symbol we want to hang on to, we must hang on to in spite of everything. You are all my friends and more than friends; you, my love and more than my love."

Awdah, you are here. Your heart beats against my palm. We have cut down so many years. Patient and methodical woodcutters, we have advanced against the jungle of time. And in our march, we ourselves have devised the tools, the arms and the compass.

We have gradually acquired the skills of navigators, water-diviners and canoeists. We have truly re-learned the skills: love, care, clarity, intelligence. All this was necessary for counteracting exile when it reared up like a beast and tried to release into our hearts the barbs of doubt, and the poison of loss. Each hard blow brought us closer together, made us straighten up, a whole person, marked out even more strikingly the fact that we belonged to each other.

So here we are, like Danko who tore his heart out of his chest and held it up to light the way for his people. Here we are outside the forest of wander-ings. With the difference that we are neither giants nor heroic saviours who can force the decisions of fate. We have only walked in step with our people. We have given according to our means and received according to our limitations. Neither of us has proved unworthy of the other. That's the essential point. Body and soul, prepared for this partaking. Now more than ever.

"Good morning."

"Good morning my love."

You open your eyes and close them immediately. You breathe a relaxed sigh. You look for my hand which I stretch out to you. I give it to you open. You take it and fall asleep again.

Back to your tale, wild-eyed sailor of the prison seas. The more you tell it, the more the spell may release its grip on you.

The warder slams the door. A blow to your heart, regular, methodical. This is the instant when prison order is uncompromising, when it shatters all the illusions it has allowed during the course of the day and which help it to fulfil its purpose: conserve in order to destroy, separate in order to maim, kill little by little so that this slow death will be judiciously recorded finally as being due to natural causes.

Boom! Clack Clack! The warder shuts the other doors in an automatic stupor. His beat over, he does another to reassure himself that the key is well and truly turned twice in the lock. He goes round again for the head-count and goes off after locking up the trusties who had stayed out to clean up the corridors.

You take a few steps in your cell. You don't think about anything. Or rather, you concentrate on one of those mental problems at which prisoners excel. Four steps by two is eight. There and back one hundred times and you can walk about half a kilometre. In one hour of walking, a thousand times there and back or four or five kilometres is quite a decent stroll.

You jump up on to your bed. You stretch out and close your eyes.

The last wave of noise rolls over the prison: someone claps his hands all alone to keep his spirits up, there are calls from one cell to another, the noise of a mess-tin being scraped, laughter, scraps of songs. Little by little, the wave dies down, collapses, then silence falls with the first advance of the tentacles of night.

You open your eyes on the ceiling-screen of your meditation. And you draw up the balance-sheet of your day. Nothing out of the ordinary in this voyage which has become as mapless as that of Christopher Columbus. Nothing with which to pad out the ship's log. It's only three days to the next visit when you will be able to fasten on to something definite, receive fresh news, refill the weekly reservoirs of emotion and of new images from which you drink each time that the greyness of prison life sticks in your throat.

You take a cigarette and light it. On the bookcase-night-table, by good luck, you come across the portrait of your wife and your children. She, sibylline, her look elusive, avoiding reality to sail on the deepest seas of memory, boring through the concentric walls of separation. They, smiling together, their cheeks shiny, ready to be kissed good-night.

You chase away the awkward questions which return to you every time you meet this look and this smile and you allow yourself to embrace the pleasant emotion which is to be rediscovered in the most common feelings. Responsibilities aside, loving one another − isn't that the most important thing?

You return to the balance-sheet of your day. Nothing out of the ordinary. Meditation. Study. Talking. The prison's an isle drifting silently around the imperceptible bend of time. Have you become a little more or a little less of a prisoner? Have you advanced or regressed in this madness to learn everything from the infinitely small to the infinitely large? What small portion did you bring to the anonymous festival of sharing? What was revealed to you in the course of your nomadic journey round the inside of your body, within the uproar of the world which submerges you in draughts swamping you like a drowning man who just manages in the nick of time to get his head out of the water and to inhale a great lungful of oxygen. Once more you are unable to reply to this great avalanche of questions. You smile at the idea of this interior voice which every evening turns itself into a kind of moral torturer and which carries out an officious harassment. Another faculty you find in yourself. Another leverage you have. You feel yourself alive.

It's the moment when you irresistibly take up one of the schoolboy notebooks in which you wrote: the title of a poem, some verses which grew without your being aware of them and which you feverishly put down on paper as if you were dealing with a meteorite which streaked across you, releasing its message as it passed, sometimes a single word which you have rolled around your mouth throughout the day and which you wrote out in capital letters as if it were the Open Sesame of the long-awaited great poem. And the terrible, blank page fills up with notes, slogans, random jottings while your spirit goes back to its source, dreams, questions, rolls and unrolls lengths of reality such as it imagines it to be and analyses it across the barriers of the long exile. Then doubts assail you. How can you give evidence from here, and more than give evidence, seize upon the nerve centre of contradictions in that turbulent flux of movement, explain precisely the suffering, the irrevocable moment when ideas are forcibly born, when history churns in the depths of the entrails of the human flood? How can you give voice to the silence of the works and days swallowed by those who have no time to lift up their eyes to see the sun set, to see the stars rise, see the splendour of the crescent moon, those who drudge in order, paradoxically, to prolong their life expectancy and to cling to the mad delusion of their species? To tell, to reproduce more intensely the diastole and systole of this immense heart that you feel gasping and heaving beyond the walls and which occasionally spurts forth the black blood of anger. Draw with authentic lines the final minutes of a child who will soon die because he bore within himself the original sin of being born on the periphery of this periphery, the indelible image of his mother poised on the edge of this distress, head hanging down, breasts empty, eyes extinguished.

You are a little like a painter who, having gone blind, succeeds after a long process of re-education in recognising colours by touch, sensitive enough to capture the least variation but who, when using canvas, feels a great anxiety because he has lost the chance of making any comparison between the fruits of his labour and the internalised model whose material existence and multiform life can only become blunted with time.

Those doubts and the great anxiety would assail you because you had always refused to be a literary bureaucrat and an exorcist of your individual ghosts. Because for you there has never been any question of shutting yourself up in a confessional to reconstitute a shadow theatre of your private hells. To write, even when you believed your cry would rise above all the others, was like a public scalping, an ordeal. You lived it and performed it with the others. The blood and the sweat of your anonymous brothers was the incense whose smoke rose from your unruly brain and allowed the "demon of poetry" to speak with your voice and to give it the timbre of popular outcry, the unbearable clamour of last judgements and of shipwrecks. To write was to collide, body against body, to march in the march. You would never get out unscathed.

War-weary, you drop your writing-book and collect the veils of your wandering imagination, you lower your eyes and look around you. This cube is your reality. Here the waters divide and meet. You will leave this millimetric space to emerge in public places and to observe the passage of the seasons and the revolution of the planets. And if you are ambitious enough to conceive of a "human comedy" it is about the small society of your prisoner friends whom you will have to separate out if you want your writing to be a real slice of the "human landscape". The power of imagination is your strength and also your weakness. So you go forward on this tightrope – hasn't your path been a succession of tightropes? And you open the floodgates of a wounded song.

You sit on your mattress, pick up your exercise book and start writing. Quickly, quickly without re-reading, without crossing out. Full stop. Date. You have reached another path up the mountain, against aphasia, against the secret wearing away of death. You have returned fire in the camp of your executioners.

Victory! You get up and stand on the low wall around the w.c. holding on to the bars of the little window. It's raining on the circular footpath. The weeds sprouting there shiver in the downpour. The sky is silent but the earth gives off a bridal smell. Your neighbour must have sensed you were at the window. He calls you.

"O.K.?"

"O.K., and you?"

"I'm well. Sing something for us."

"Not now. I must write letters."

"Give everyone my best wishes."

"I will."

You remain for a moment, breathing in the disturbing smell of the earth, then you get down. You re-read the letters which arrived that morning. Real voices are now speaking to you. The walls of the cell disappear. An overwhelming sense of actuality. You ask yourself how it's possible, so much love, all these kinds of human warmth. Is it the prison which makes you overvalue one another and which encloses inside itself excessive feelings, or is it rather something which we have inside ourselves, within us, and which re-emerges in this way because the ordeal has allowed us to break down our internal walls and to tear up our winding-sheet of old world defects?

"Tomorrow the visit . . . To be there with you, with you all, feel the spirit of comradeship which is the most important symbol we want to hang on to, we must hang on to in spite of everything. You are all my friends and more than friends; you, my love and more than love."

So you pick up the sheet of writing-paper. You fill out the head of the sheet reserved for information: name, date, number, remand or sentenced (you resist the futile gesture). You put the process of self-conservation into gear and renew the lexicon of symbolism to be used so that this very simple communication does not "get lost", but also so that your anger is conveyed without its wings being clipped. The page, a single page to record the happenings of a few days, to communicate the fruits of your folly and your wisdom, your hopes and your dreams, bottles in the water and dated testaments that you send off, fragile seeds of sharing. You should act a little like Proteus, form your thoughts and your enthusiasms into the same size as this page, not a line more or less. You write as small as possible. You get the maximum benefit from the smallest space. You are like those old scribes from the days when writing was a rare and holy act, even dangerous:

My beloved, I was not able to write to you yesterday evening as I had intended, and I went to sleep convinced that I would receive a letter from you in the morning. I was not wrong. This morning your lovely, sweet letter of the 15th . . . A good place to say that I like your letters, your news, which are moving to me in the extreme . . . A great confidence in us and in the future. The account of everyday deeds and actions which entranced me as if it were a fairy-tale. I am incurable, you see. I put an extremely high price on that which would only be routine in a normal life. But if I look at it and see it like that, it's because I see much of the future in my imagination, we two woven into this routine, the sweet amazement of recovered freedom, all bars banished, exiled in their turn from our horizon and that of our people. Hope like a permanent cry, the promises of life, confidence in justice, the arrival of all those possibilities glimpsed during the course of our struggles.

I understand what you want to say in your letter: it is true, it's difficult to be a woman (a whole woman, that's to say equal but superior to men by virtue of all those perspectives upon which she calls with all her strength as she feels more strongly the chains of oppression). In this way, in a society

73

like ours, to be a woman or to be a prisoner is a bit the same. From this arise our similarities, our lively fraternity and our bizarre happiness.

Writing to you is like a shot of oxygen to my brain. It breathes better. The whirlpool moves off a bit. Keeps away. Near to you, my beloved, speaking to you. It's terrible to have sometimes to repress life within oneself. That is what happened to me a few days ago. Now I let it rise up again as I hear you, as I call to you. Pick off the scabs of silence. Talk to release happiness. I don't know if you understand me. It's as if there were new, interiorised hells that I need to "exorcise". And when one is conscious of all that is involved in this game, it's even more difficult. "I pass", as someone used to say.

Depressing to think about our wonderful country which is made to delude the hopes of men. This protracted blood-letting, grief imposed on life. Now we have really to overcome the slow death, free the sources of life and unchain the sun. Our country will recover its colours, recover its health and will distribute armfuls of happiness . . .

More and more the urge to write. A huge poem will have space for the body of our "mad sphinx of a sun", a poem which crosses the continent of History, which mobilises the collective memory, which allows a glimpse of the future accumulated in our unhappy present . . .

The need to be with you for a little while. A pity you cannot read me simultaneously. This is the evening, when I write most frequently, to be sure you get my letters by the end of the morning. How are you my love? What bad luck to have the dreadful 'flu. You will laugh at me but I must tell you something: when I see you are ill, my first reaction is one of anger. I know that's not fair. It's as if someone had played a dirty trick on me.

As for me I have decided to take a course of anti-rheumatism treatment, for that was giving me trouble a few days ago. Yesterday I had a hard time. Today it's a lot better. You see, these rheumatics never leave me alone. In order to have some control I will have to get used again to a more intense level of pain. I shall do that.

I dream a lot lately, threatened dreams, wandering, beset by obstacles, but beautiful, restorative glimpses of your presence. So, yesterday, I dreamed about Qods. She was on my knee, I was teasing her, laughing with her like a madman. Did you realise that dreams end up by creating certain atmospheres, turning familiar places into something new. It's like that for me, there are some places I always go back to, a kind of farm near some caves by the sea, a large Moroccan house which reminds me both of the Alhambra and one of the houses I used to live in, in Fes, a kind of apartment in a building but open to the sky with doorless rooms. For the most part these places are only different combinations of the same prison-space. Not always, for in some of the dreams I don't feel completely affected by this space. All the same, the capacity to dream is prodigious. And so important for a prisoner.

You know, ever since I have been alone in my cell, you are more present than ever. Unlike when I was sharing, I am more free in my thoughts and day-dreams. When one is alone one is always a bit mad. Sometimes one makes a remark without realising, or one laughs, one can sing without asking permission, one has serious discussions with oneself or with an imaginary companion. Solitude is a peculiarly peopled condition. All this is to say that I speak to you at great length.

There we are. There's no more room left to write. So good-night, my beloved. I give you my hand. Kiss our children.

Your letter finished, you stretch out again on the mattress. You have no desire to read. Today you are still observing the "reading strike" you embarked upon a few days ago. This happens to you from time to time when you feel tired of other people's voices, however close or fraternal they may be. You need to decant into yourself these different languages, let them merge or separate with your own voice, find their own way to a fusion or rejection in your melting-pot. To read in this condition is a form of alienation or a life by proxy. You therefore refused all diversions, all help which was not information or raw material which you uprooted with your own hands from the Russian mountains you are exploring, looking for your faults.

You get down from the mattress and go to the door. You call the warder. Finally he comes.

"Put the light out please."

"You want to go to sleep?"

"Yes."

He closes the judas and puts out the light. You go back to bed, cover yourself, your eyes open.

Prison night. How immense and true you are. The

language of silence by decree. You do not hide, no, you reveal more truly the subtle alienations, the scars of genocide, legal and otherwise. In you flourishes the unpardonable song, human and earthly, which will only be extinguished with the last of the just. In you the song will be forever; it will not die.

Night-womb, earth warm in its roots which spread, spread, gorged with sap and blood, indefatigable creators of the spring to come, of the great festival of the poor.

Sleep, sleep well number 18 611. Your day is over. Deep down you know that you have not wasted your time.

Whatever of us died in the ripples of exile
look at me now on the threshold of learning
everything amazes me
the earth
rebelling against night
pushing men
into the whirlpool of apathy
O my sad one
the lover of my powerful dreams
when will I again be able
to spell out the letters
of my rude name.

4.

The full blast of the street. You give your hand to your wife for this first dip into the crowd.

You walk like any other of freedom's porters, oblivious of their precious cargo. You feel none too steady on your legs. Your body pitches slightly. You feel again that spray-seasoned dizziness which heralds sea-sickness as the unsettled gulls throw out their eerie cry in every direction.

A warm wind smelling of seaweed and the musk of pollen overwhelms you, stings your nostrils, your eyelids and collects in every pore of your face. You open your hand, seize a fistful of the odour and put it in your pocket. Sleep-walking in daylight, you do not distinguish passers-by too well. The crowd's still in a state of nebulous motion where hundreds of eyes glimmer. You have the impression that all those eyes are fixed on you, hostile, lazy, bewildered. They ceaselessly measure you from head to foot, swarm around the nape of your neck, survey the whole length of your backbone, spin round, attack your stomach and then seize and pull the hairs of your beard. Hostile, lazy, bewildered eyes. They undress you as if they wanted to examine this body of yours, see into the depths of your soul, follow the contours and shape of this pain with which you are assumed to be tattooed even in your most intimate places.

You try not to meet these looks, to make yourself very small in your wife's hand and in your new civilian clothes. But those very clothes accentuate your incongruity. For even though they are dark blue and soberly cut, you think they are too revealing, that they mould you too closely, that they give you a Sunday-best, peacockish air. You still do not wear them as you used to wear your prison uniform. The brown cloth uniform in winter, the striped canvas in summer, yours and those of your fellow prisoners were a unifying force. It was the origin of the feeling which took hold of you when you sat down in the exercise yard with your back to the wall and settled down to look at your comrades as they walked around. Their clothing no longer held your attention. You could see them better, smile at the temperament of each one which revealed itself in the simplest way in the world – in his demeanour, his way of holding his arms, the theatrical gestures which accompanied his speech and his automatic comings and goings.

A blast from a car horn puts an end to your day-dream, and your wife pulls you firmly back to let a car pass. You discover the aggressive round of traffic. The cars go at an abnormal speed. Whirling and scattering in every direction, they remind you of the dodge'ms in fairs of the dim and distant past. The street is like a battlefield. Pedestrians and motorists are given over to a war of strategies and attrition. He who manoeuvres best is the one who gets first place in the opposing lines.

You get across as best you can, rejoin the mass which

stretches along the pavement of the great avenue. You still aren't managing to look straight ahead, to well and truly meet those eyes, and challenge them to find another object for their curiosity.

You lift up your head to cast a look over the whole perspective of the avenue. The large buildings reassume one by one their places in your revitalised memory. Bank, Post Office, railway station, Courts of Justice and right at the bottom a minaret, like a watchtower lording it over these new arrivals. You can't remember whether this minaret used to be there or at least if it used to be so clearly visible. It is possible that the avenue has been widened, that some buildings have been demolished to improve the perspective and to bring about this special realignment which is desirable as a faithful reflection of the other realignments which have been created in your country during your absence. As ever your attention is especially focussed on the examples of colonial-moorish architecture. It is here that Lyautey had succeeded in imparting to his urban engineers a moral which had proved useful elsewhere. *Show your power so as not to have to use it* was the motto. Public buildings had to inspire in each citizen the feeling of the power of the State and of its continuity. No capricious decorations which could be interpreted as weaknesses in the System, but a reminder that this State was a product of a grafting and that in order that this graft should take well it was necessary to preserve something of the original plant, even if only at the level of local material, local colour, of a graphic symbolism whose significance had become more and more hazy for the natives themselves.

In spite of that, you feel a tightening in your heart at seeing again those ambiguous buildings which have successfully survived so many social cataclysms including your own without anyone ever thinking of questioning their use and their continued place in the scenery of everyday life. The world is like that, you say to yourself. Men are like that, these products of successive graftings who struggle for the whole of their lives to reinstate a space of original purity even though this effort pushes them even deeper into multiplicity.

Sleep-walking in daylight you carve out a path for yourself in the heart of the mass. A vague disquiet overtakes you. Who is to say that this provisional liberty is not a prelude to your actual death sentence? It will be necessary now for you to learn to take account of many factors of which surely not the least is the absurd. You know very well not to dramatise, that you are not as yet the Demon King whose elimination would bring peace to the Masters of the Moment or to the sorcerer's apprentices who grow big in their shadow and fatten themselves with scraps. But at the moment you are not capable of reasoning calmly and serenely as you used to do when you were in your cell at the most critical moments of your prison history. There, the concentric circles all around you (doors, doorways, bars, iron gates, iron bars, walls, high walls, warden, administrators, watch guards, control towers) could be regarded para-doxically as a safety barrier. You knew very well that this barrier was not there to protect you but to protect society from you, protect the fertile compost of hopes and ideas, the misery of hunger and anger.

"...never came to see you at the house, did he?" ...more than he came to see you there, I suppose ...conspiratorial smile of amusement and bit... You will have to submit to other greetings... ...kind. Unless you go into exile again, but this ti... ...desert island.

...o you are once again claimed by your prisons. T... ...inful sensations aroused by the encounter d... ...wn. You return to the contemplation of this grea... ...venue, and that, without rhyme or reason, takes yo... ...o the citadel of exile. You remember a game which ...you and your comrades used to play during the ...endless, sleepless evenings.

For the most part, you organised these evenings after the weekly visit. You used to be too unsettled by the reunions, by the gusts of freedom which had blown over you from the other side of the grill, the fresh news, the renewed declarations, the words of affection exchanged, the light in the eyes into which you had gazed tenderly. You were really incapable of going back to your books, your studies and your lonely meditations. You all felt the need for contact and confidences, playful activities, songs, dreams spoken out loud. You also used to make a feast with the food that your families had brought, special dishes which they knew you particularly liked, fresh salads, fruits in season, juice and even pastries and other tasty delicacies which you divided into equal portions and for which you drew lots (some ate them right away, others ate a bit of them or kept them all to offer to the children on the next visit). Eating was part of the festivities, it was not a routine matter, a moment of silence while one chewed one's ration

But all the same you found there a way of coming to terms with your own death. You could discuss it concretely, in analytical terms, as a function of the breath of life which was in you and whose intensity you could evaluate at every moment. The problem never presented itself to you as a metaphysical one. The disquiet, the great disquiet, had its basis in other subjects: this country which continued to ride the waves of its misery and its recurrent rebellion in spite of your absence and your own errors when you sincerely believed you could change the world by will-power and when you used to look at the citadel of savagery as a house of cards that a rallying cry would bring down, your silent adventure with poetry which used to carry you to the edge of madness. Then too, the idea that you would one day be free, and how you would experience it, how everything that was gathered inside you (warmth, questions, new layers of will, the mature fruits of your ordeal) would be able to find a way forward towards realisation and would not collide against other stubborn realities impossible to determine in advance. Yes, your death was a problem sorted out, or at least you were able to pronounce on that subject when the need made itself felt and to analyse it as a concrete situation.

But now, in the flabby belly of this mass through which you were making your way, chance was king. Death could strike you like nature in one of her caprices. At least that was how you felt.

You start again, rid yourself of this game of Russian dolls which is boxed into your brain and emerge from the mist of associations. You turn to your wife. She smiles.

"Do you find it changed?"

"No, not much."

You decide in the end to look at the passers-by, to stare them in the eye, to hold out to the end against the iron-handed adversary. Men, women and children, mostly young, hardly any old people. You feel rather stupid as you become aware of this. You already knew this reality, statistics showed it. The youth of the population and the problems it presents for teaching, employment, leisure; the effects of all that on the evolution of ideas, behaviour and politics. But it's not exactly these considerations which occupy you at that moment. You satisfy yourself in giving free rein to looking around yourself. You try to control the crowd and to decipher it. You look at bodies, faces, actions. You listen so that you can capture bits of conversations and tones of voice. How can one know what is going on in the head of this crowd, all at the same time? Not the thought of each passer-by, his cares, the internal dialogue he develops while walking but the shared basis or rather the outcome of these multitudes of shattered thoughts which whirl around above their heads like bubbles in cartoon drawings. How can one tell, by the enigmatic smile of one person, the surly look of another, the absent air of a third, what are the ideas circulating, whether they converge or diverge, those which will lead to something happening and those which will get lost in the unacknowledged morass of the unsayable, in the cloud of still-born thought? And in this search you know you cannot make use of guidelines outside your own body as seismograph, your eyes as probe. So, finally, you are living that cliché of "bathing in the crowd".

"It's not possible!"

Both the voice and the gest[ure] [...] attention are familiar. You li[...] from the other side of the grave[...] and pfft! throws you the faded [...] and a synopsis of things which h[...] shipwreck. You still can't put a na[me...] you know what it's all about and a[...] already assessed the weight of the c[...] used to be between you.

"*Al Hamdullah 'ala assalamah!* (Tha[nks] for returning you safely.) I'm very h[appy to see] you."

"Thank you, thank you."

The man has already put his arm around y[ou...] you on both cheeks and breathed warmly o[n your] neck. You let him. You are not brave eno[ugh to] crudely disentangle yourself from these emb[races.] You have always had this scrupulous reverenc[e for] the dignity of the other, whoever he may be.

"You have not changed at all."

"Really?" you reply for the sake of something to say.

"Oh, yes, yes, it's true. A few more grey hairs, bu[t] that's all. You look in good health."

"You as well," you reply, rather disconcerted.

"Good, I'll leave you. I'll come to see you. Still at the same address?"

You acknowledge this fact.

"Well, once again, I'm very happy to see you. Wonderful!" he exclaims while almost jumping as he turns his back on you and disappears into the crowd. You take your wife's hand again and continue your walk, silent for a moment.

absent-mindedly. It was a ceremony of sharing. You took upon yourself the care which had presided over the preparation of each dish, the choice of this vegetable or this fruit, the hands and the eyes of those dearest to you were recollected in the aroma which you could recognise amongst a thousand, or more simply by this plate or the basin which had come from out there, and the sight of which turned you into a traveller outside prison-time. Once the supper was over, one of you made tea. The one in charge or a volunteer would clean the floor. A third washed up. Tea was served, you formed a circle and the evening began. News, stories, gossip, but you soon gave up being serious and gave way to laughter, to the mockery which only arises among people who have got to know one another in the most intimate way, in the smallest details of each other's personalities, habits, tics, weak points, contradictions, deficiencies. In this game there are always fall-guys, less gifted than others in repartee, in the act of getting their own back. But in general everyone ended up by suffering his share of caricature which he either took in good part or bridled over.

As the evening wore on you would abandon the present and the directly observable in favour of sailing on the rough sea of memory. Song inflated the sails of nostalgia. You became the twins of those Volga boatmen or those wanderers of the Russian steppe that Gorky and Sholokhov had made you love. In turn you sang as well, in all the languages that you knew, you turned the Tower of Babel on its head.

The beautiful voice of the prisoners' cell rising from the heart of the citadel of exile, piercing through the soft shell of the night, flying from cell to cell, from wing to wing, bumping against the watchtowers, a lyrical comet leaving for the stars which shone more beautifully as they received this prayer from another earth age.

But you knew instinctively when you should break off from this nostalgia, put your feet on the ground, release the mischievous cascade of laughter. Jokes smouldered again, mockery started up again.

"Tell me then, A., this girl who came to see you today, she's not even a member of your family."

"It's true. I've never even seen her before."

"But all the same, he smiled at her in a very familiar way."

"The girl was also making eyes at him."

A. withdraws, he has a half-stupid, half-serious smile on his lips.

"I tell you, there was nothing out of the ordinary," he says finally with a thick tongue.

"Certainly nothing out of the ordinary. But I believe you had a certain understanding."

"So what? We discussed a lot of things," replied A.

"That's for sure, you discussed the problem of women's liberation. And you suggested to her that you go deeper into the subject the next time."

"And go still deeper when you get out."

Everyone laughs.

"You animals," shouts A. and laughs, defeated.

"The animal sleeps in all of us," someone replies, mercilessly.

More laughter.

Do you know the latest Babani (popular fool) joke?" says B.

"O.K., tell us."

"Well, Babani was learning French. The teacher asked him to conjugate the verb *aller* in the present indicative. Babani hesitated. The teacher gave him a smack.

" 'Alright. I'll start and you continue. *Je vais à Marrakech . . .* Now?' And Babani followed up with: '*Tu vas à Tarrakech. Il va à Sarrakech . . .*' "

"Someone told me a good one today," C. puts forward.

"Yes?"

"It's the story of the parrot with the long tongue. Its owner had arranged his perch on the balcony directly over the street. The parrot, which had a sharp sense of observation, abused passers-by all day long. He had a particular taste for a policeman whose beat took him past there every day. Not being able to stand any more of the bird's insults, the policeman decided one day to speak to the owner:

" 'If you don't shut your parrot up, you'll have me to deal with.'

"The owner was left in no doubt as to the policeman's intentions. He took the parrot and threw him in the hen-run. As soon as the parrot appeared, the hens ran around in a panic. They gathered together at the bottom of the run and looked at one another in terror as they glanced at the new arrival. Finally the parrot called to them in a haughty tone: 'What's the matter with you cowards. Haven't you ever seen a political prisoner?' "

"I've got another," says C.

"Let me tell mine," says D.

"I have a very short one," suggests E.

89

The wave of laughter rises, breaks and crashes over the walls of the cell and flies into pieces. Other waves come and unite with them from other cells. The prison guffaws with an open throat and this colossal laugh bursts like the gunpowder of defiance. In the walkways of the corridors, in the control towers, the sentries must be sad. Their guns hang from their shoulders like those sheep's jawbones with which children play at street cowboys-and-Indians during the nights of Ramadan.

But the laughter itself can become unbearable. By instinct you learn when to cut it short, to sense the moment when its aim is not restricted to the boils which infect life's backside, the accumulated miseries of the poor, the widespread stupidity of a hostile surveillance system, the moment, that is, when it overshoots all that and threatens to bespatter your sense of life and your own self. The grotesque without limits is neighbour to the absurd.

Therefore you pre-empted it and the laughter would die away little by little. Then you would organise a space for recollections. Each one would tell of his personal experiences, his family history, his apprenticeships and his first and last loves. You accepted spontaneously the rules of the truth game. You divested yourself of your social and political character, you became a story among a thousand others, of suffering, of inner struggle, of obstacles, but all the same it was a remarkable journey. And you knew that this game was neither dangerous nor arbitrary. By accepting it, you were still sharing, you were tearing yourself away from your narrowness

90

and you were relieving for each other the burden of internal walls. The gift was your transparency.

But memory was also a slippery slope which led you gradually to rock bottom, that time you had passed in the hidden torture chambers before reaching official prisons. You might digress, but you got there all the same, to the experience which obsessed you all and which would obsess you for a long time yet. There memory became an incredible precision instrument. You remembered the smallest gesture, the least word, the most horrific situations and the most magnificent ones. But the curious thing was that when you spoke about it you did not do so in a solemn or serious voice. You reconstituted this experience in cartoon form. From all the small daily tragedies of which you had been witnesses or hero/victims you strove to extract the ingredients of comedy. It was not the mechanical crushing of a living being which was the source of your laughter. You had turned the proposition upside down. It was rather the living being shouting out for self-expression from within the sinister machine which was the source of your comic energy. Each one would tell his story. The place of torture was turned into a stage of miracles where two opposing classes (prisoners and *houjjajs*) gave themselves over to a merciless war in the manner of Tom and Jerry. The *houjjajs* (the keepers of these places) had the role of arranging hunger, filth, silence, preventing communications, distributing punishments with a kind of weird fairness, supporting the sub-human order of the reign of terror. They used, in carrying out these tasks, an ingenuity without equal except that displayed by the prisoners in their turn, to get hold of pitiful supplements to their tiny rations, find out about the place, communicate with each other, get snippets of information about the outside world, fight against vermin, rats and gloom. All that went on while the coming-and-going to the interrogation chambers never stopped and while there arose night and day from the neighbouring cellars the cries of suffering. The war went on. With the tenacity of ants the prisoners had humanised their open graves, made them somewhere liveable, a court of miracles in the most powerful sense of the phrase.

"Where are we heading for?"

"The Oudayas, would you like that?"

"Oh, yes."

Hey, sleepwalker, wake up! Leave your double for the moment. Open your eyes. What's before you here and now, this medina you have just entered, and this other crowd which is more tightly packed, so different from that of the grand boulevards because it is squeezed into narrow, little streets, wallowing in the noise and the perfumes, these choruses of blind beggars holding out wooden bowls, intoning prayers of suffering and pity, these unlicensed traders who like the guerillas of poverty play hide-and-seek with the police auxiliaries, these loitering little boys with oversized heads and bulging eyes who offer you plastic bags, Jex pads, wash-gloves, these youths (boys and girls) stopped in front of shops with cassettes by Bob Marley, the Egyptian propagandist Kichk, the Jil Jilala group, the comic Bziz and Baz, the singer Rouicha . . . The call of the muezzins which has just reverberated and causes a group of the faithful to

92

hurry towards the mosques, this female tourist in shorts and low-cut blouse who strolls around at the height of Ramadan under the furious but powerless gaze of the haughty shop-keepers, this greengrocer or butcher whose glance meets yours and who gives you an enigmatic smile, first step towards a recognition which will need other meetings before becoming effective and freeing the tongue, opening the hand to greet the Return . . .

Wake up sleepwalker! Everything you see here is real as well. It is here that you will have to live from now on if you want to slough off the zombie.

Yes, you understand that. You have opened your eyes as wide as possible. You see, sense and feel at a distance. You register, you register like the hi-fidelity instrument that you have always been. You lose nothing of the street, of the crowd, of the smells, of the noise. Honestly, you are not absent. But whatever you do cannot retrieve the foot that you somehow left in the citadel of exile, you cannot disconnect your thoughts from there, from the mass of images which your past prison life still sends forth. You are power-less against this capacity or this deformity for being everywhere at once which is fixed like a third eye on your forehead. The solitary palm-tree of the prison's central courtyard appears before you, takes the place of the minaret which you were staring at a moment ago. Its dishevelled top rattles in the wind. Where were you now?

Yes. You had started off looking at the long avenue. And this had taken you to the prison and the memory of the game with which you, your comrades and yourself, amused yourselves during the long evenings.

Then one thing led to another and you reconstituted the course of a whole evening. No, it is not you who are responsible for the wave-like motion which carries off your story, there's no question of lending yourself to the contrivances of the art of digression. On the contrary you have the feeling that the story already has its form while still inside you, like the fruit of your womb. So then your role consists in bringing it to term, most naturally, without having recourse to the forceps or Caesarian section. It is enough for you to follow its beat, its ebb and flow, in order to recover the texture of life in its natural complexity. In this way by successively drawing closer and listening, by agreeable contractions, if one wants to push the comparison that far, you finally give birth to something both familiar and unique and project it into the glaring light of communication.

But let's go back to this game. After all that you have recounted, does it still have some significance? Has it not already served its purpose in relieving your overflowing memory? Perhaps.

This qualification is admitted and the palm tree witness vanishes as quickly as it had appeared. The minaret resumes its place before your eyes. You are struck by its simple beauty, its calm. The call of the muezzin is over. And the noise of the medina rises up again. The minaret acts like a pump which sucks up the noise and drives it, scatters it into the depths of the blue sky.

You are still holding your wife's hand and you both continue to cut your way through the crowd in the same shared, meditative silence. To walk like that fills you with a pleasure which has something of the erotic

94

in it. A fullness. This crowd is so different from that of the grand boulevards: not the same crowd. Gone is the swarm of hostile eyes. To walk in the crowd is to make contact, body to body. The burnous of a passer-by slips and catches on your hand a bit, the fold of a jellaba wraps round your leg, you feel against yourself the pressure of a shoulder, of a hip, a breast. You have just enough time to press yourself against a wall so that you are not crushed by a donkey going rapidly past. If you jostle someone or are jostled, neither of you engages in any polite formulas, you continue on your way, with an expression of understanding.

For the moment you take no notice of your tendency to overvalue such things. You savour this waking dream which has plunged you into the rude but hospitable body of your people.

You emerge from the medina and go back up the little slope which leads to the Kasbah of the Oudayas. Before entering the gardens you quickly think over what you will find. A curious intellectual habit, doubtless shared by many, which means one does not respect the normal process of knowing and recognising. One does not want to discover or rediscover things in a direct way. This means that the way one looks at things or looks around places is conditioned by a preconceived image and by the emotional charge which one has worked up in advance. The result: things are seen through two superimposed visions. Is this a bad thing, or a good one?

You step across the threshold of the garden and instinctively turn your head to the left. You know what is there, a bit above ground level: a small, blue door embedded in the wall. Yes, it's still there, repainted, resplendent with an enormous pattern, half-floral and half-geometric. But you notice this time that the door does not lead anywhere. There is no house and no shop behind it. It's merely a small recess in the wall. It seems to be there simply to please the eye.

You go down a few steps and the garden is spread before you. But the chain-pump which used to be there, on the left, does not work any more. The donkey which used to turn it has disappeared. You notice for the first time that the trees and flowers which used to thrive here are not simply beautiful perfumed plants, as you used to see them in the past. You now recognise bougainvilleas, thorn-apple, jacaranda, and you know how to tell the difference between zinnias and dahlias, here are sweet-peas, there snap-dragons. The garden is no longer a place to pass through, it is a continent where there co-exist in a most peaceful harmony species which each have their individuality, their rhythm of growth and each of which occupies its needed space without recourse to the violent jealousy of the human species. Here is another continent which prison revealed to you.

You enter the café, take a seat. The décor has not changed but the tables have been repainted a turquoise blue. Also the stork's nest which used to be on top of the wall has disappeared. The gnarled fig-tree whose trunk used to offer clefts like vaginas has lost all its leaves. It looks like a shaky old man, resting on his stick. In the other direction, the sea has ebbed a little and numerous seagulls are foraging about and fluttering on the beach.

The old waiter who used to come running each

96

time you came here, welcoming you and giving you the title *Fqih* does not even notice your presence. He's dozing, half-leaning near the café's kitchen. You finally wake him from his sleep by signalling and calling quietly. He gets up unhurriedly, rising painfully on his legs, and lurches over to you. He casts a cursory glance over you and your wife. You exchange glances with this face from before the deluge in your little life. Unrecognisable. That's it then, eight years: these pupils half-covered by a greyish film, these lips cracked and distended which open to rev·al a largely toothless mouth, this hunched back and these shaking legs, and then above all this, the dull voice which finally emerges from a black hole in the middle of the face and which asks you, showing no surprise and with no title:

"What do you want to drink?"

"Two mint teas."

The waiter departs on the same unsteady legs, leaving your hand to return to your pocket, the hand you had got ready to offer him to renew your erstwhile friendship, which you had wanted to rediscover as you had rediscovered a while ago the little door of painted wood.

"I don't like this feeling."

"Which?"

"I have the sensation of being a tourist."

The old waiter returns with two glasses of tea smoking on a plate. You smile and look him in the eye. He looks at you as well with a puzzled air. You finally say:

"You don't recognise me?"

"Certainly," he replies, for the sake of saying something. "It's a long time since we last saw you."

"It's true, it's a long time."

"A long journey, overseas perhaps?"

He pronounces "overseas" with a great deal of emphasis, drawing out the syllables.

"Yes, something like that. A long journey."

"'ala assalamah, " he says finally, taking the coins you had put on the table. Then he goes off to serve other customers.

"Why a tourist?"

"Because I'm feeling everything still from the outside. People, things, that unreal sea over there, this man who does not recognise me. More than that, I feel a stranger in my own body."

"What about me?"

"You are my umbilical cord, you are the voice and the body of my slow, slow resurrection."

You begin to sip your tea and your eyes meet at some point where the horizon merges with the sea. You are sure that she is going to say "I love you". So you take hold of her hand and before she can speak you say:

"Me too."

"Shall we go?"

"O.K."

You have just got up when a group of tourists invade the café. A dozen quite elderly men and women. The guide explains about the place in English, arranges for drinks to be served, allocates the new arrivals to vacant tables. He behaves like a despot in charge of slightly backward children. His troop cackles and obeys. Cameras point in all directions. Wonderful! Always the same hackneyed cliché! You are still in the garden.

"I would like to phone up G. Then I'd like to go

back home and hear you play the guitar."

"O.K. What are these flowers called?"

"I don't know."

"They are volubilis. I like them very much. You see, your culture still needs some working on."

You go back into the medina. Rue des Consuls. Souk Sebbat. Souiqa. The same tumult, the same smells, the same generosity in the action of walking. But what now captures your attention is people's demeanour. You would expect, knowing of the poverty, the chronic repression, the despair of idle hands, all the things you knew before you were snatched out of the bath of life, and what you have learned since from books, statistics, the stories of your visitors, to see passers-by present a miserable and defeated mask marked by the shedding of invisible tears, but not for you, statistician of sorrow and chronicler of attacks on life. You had imagined that people would be more worn out not only in their collective consciousness but also their appearance, their way of walking, of raising and lowering their heads. You would have expected to see the signs of rebellion and of anger marked on the face of each one of life's disinherited. In fact, you notice nothing like that. So at least from this point of view you have the feeling you have not been away. You find the same good nature, the same smile ready to flower, the same lively emotions expressed on each face. Fatalism? Cultural temperament? There's a little of that. But you feel convinced that that is not the essential element. At the most profound levels of your culture you know that this behaviour has its roots in the self-control dictated by an uncrushable conviction of dignity. And, deep in the history of this country, a symbiosis which nothing can impair between the people and the land: enjoyment of all its aspects, the resultant native genius which bursts forth in great explosions of song, at once lyrical and rational, as well as in drawing, dance, poetry and in everything which makes up the ineradicable voice of this people. So you tell yourself that it's so much the better that people do not wear masks, so much the better that they show this enigmatic endurance, so much the better that they do not allow their oppressors to see the image of their defeat or weakness, and so much the better that they hide beneath their skin the yeast of future awakenings.

Once through the medina you find yourself again on the grand boulevard. From one world to another. "Land of contrasts", as is often parroted by those who wish to lure the sun-worshippers into the trap of a country where "nature has remained natural". And it's true, one can read the truth of this proposition behind all appearances. One only has to cross this town from one side to the other to realise the deep sickness of the country and its people, to touch upon the outrages which only cause mild insomnia amongst impotent moralists and philosophers who erect their systems like pyramids so as to give the illusion that they have a more advantageous over-view. This town is like a suppurating sore which is spreading and for which cosmetic surgery can do nothing. So you are walking now on an open wound. You can't stop yourself from getting out your rebel's sword. It's difficult for you to drag your feet across this unwieldy city which imprisons the future and nourishes itself with inequality and starvation.

The shops stretch out, newspaper kiosks, cafés. These cafés for men are sinister places where the idlers, their ostentation reeking of emptiness, scan the sports pages, while endlessly scribbling on score sheets for cards or lotto, noisily slurping every five minutes from their large glasses of white coffee. No woman may pass without being fastened with leech-like gazes square on her buttocks or sexual triangle; few lift their eyes to look at the face of this ephemerally coveted object. All the while at their feet, the small, hairy shoe-shine boys who have difficulty in awakening them from their doubtful reveries when they have finished polishing and want to be paid.

You stop at a newspaper kiosk. Showcase of that smart democracy the loudspeakers are pleased to present as a model for the countries of the Third World. And it's true that everything can be found in this kiosk, or practically everything. Swamp quality by quantity, take the edge off the appetite by overloading it, suffocate interest by encouraging the inflation of information, that seems to be the logic which is hidden by this show which finally deceives no one except the casual passer-by. In underdevelopment the peripheries of democracy resemble a shadow theatre which allows some élites to give the illusion that they can fulfil the roles assigned to them by history. In this way they ignore what's going on behind the scenes and the real actors, whom they only see as silhouettes right up until the day when social cataclysms come and blow down this pasteboard theatre, carrying off these painted scenes and their shadows, burying these illusions until the next masquerade.

"Don't forget that you wanted to phone."

You go into the Post Office and go towards the telephone cubicles. You dial the number. Two or three rings and someone lifts up the receiver at the other end.

"Hello!"

You recognise the voice of your friend abroad.

"Is that you, G?"

"Yes."

"Guess who's speaking?"

"It's impossible! I thought I was dreaming. I don't know what to say."

"I didn't phone you to say anything. It's just for the being, the sharing."

"Great. You're O.K. How do you feel?"

"Still disoriented. You know, it's as if there had been a fire in my head. In all my senses. It will take time before I re-emerge and re-occupy my body and my voice, really have my eyes open."

"And Awdah?"

"Splendid."

"And the others, those who are still inside?"

"No news at the moment. We're still waiting. It would be great if this small hope turned into a big one."

"I still can't believe that you are at the other end of the line. But all the same your voice is there, entirely. The telephone is a wonderful instrument."

"Yes, wonderful. Listen, I'll write to you. We'll write won't we?"

"Yes, we'll write. All my love, and to Awdah."

"All my love as well. Good-bye."

"Good-bye."

You go to the counter. Ask how much the call cost. Get out the money to pay. At this precise moment you feel a disturbing presence, but it's not like someone looking at you fixedly without your knowing until it reaches the point where you finally look up instinctively or turn around to see what's going on. What you feel now is different, a sort of cold current full of disturbing vibrations which seize you round the waist, turning into a warm bristling which rises out of your stomach, kneading your heart, crosses your lungs and comes out through your eyes which begin to grow hazy.

Come on, old salt of the prison seas. You know what is going on. You have smelled a smell which is *sui generis* ; like a transfixed animal, you sense the body capable of giving off this cold current. The years have not blunted this sixth sense that allows you to nose out danger from a distance, to recognise your human antagonist. Even before you lift your eyes you know what is going on. You turn around slowly and your gaze meets that of the man who is half-leaning at the other end of the counter. But the surprise is still great. This is not just any Guardian of Prosperity. He who turned his eyes away when he knew you were looking at him is none other than the black giant. By his demeanour you are certain that he is there by chance, that it has got nothing to do with any kind of duty. He is attending to his affairs like any other anonymous passer-by whose only concern is to get it over with as quickly as possible. You realise that his

103

back has become bent and his hair has turned grey. The result of eight years in any man's life? All the same you now remember a detail of your interrogation. Among the arguments which the giant put forward to persuade you to speak as quickly as possible there was the fact that he was in a hurry to get home because it was the Feast of the Sacrifice. And he would not be able to sacrifice the sheep, enjoy himself with his children if he had not done his job, had not got out of you what his boss had asked him to get. All of a sudden he attempted uselessly to make you feel guilty because of religious duty. You were, on top of everything else, a spoil-sport and an obstacle to innocent children being together with their father, enjoying themselves on this day as was the right of all Muslim children.

You smile as you remember this grotesque episode. Curious, you say to yourself. Even in the most inhuman acts one can discern characteristic traits, a cultural specificity.

You pay for your call, turn your back on this apparition from another epoch. You are now sure that the giant is looking after you. You walk away with the same sense you had when you were going backwards and forwards between the torture chamber and the bare cell where they took you from time to time so that you could reflect and recover. You once again take your wife's arm and she senses what you are feeling:

"What's the matter?"

"There, behind us, the black giant."

"What black giant?"

"One of those evil genies who snatched me away

from you one day, or perhaps his ghost."

"Are you sure?"

"Just as one can sometimes be sure of having lived a previous existence."

You leave the Post Office and head for home. You allow yourself to be guided by your wife without seeing or understanding anything. You resemble a bee-keeper who has put on his protective mask and who pokes his head into a dark hive the size of a condemned cell, or an Oedipus from a time when tragedy is so banal that you could go blinded through the streets and attract less attention than a car accident. You are suddenly unsteady on your legs. You start to limp while the pain mounts through your body, becoming less and less physical. You think about this shipwreck of a country, drifting between change and permanence, between the tricks of history and the favoured agents of history. Your ideas are in a turmoil. You feel yourself inside the skin of an adolescent who has just been expelled from school and who looks in astonishment at the improbable cog-wheels of the vast social machine into which he will have to put his fingers, at the risk of having them crushed.

"So will you play your guitar?"

"What do you want me to sing?"

"Anything you like."

On your return you had immediately rushed into the bathroom and run the hot water. You had washed yourself meticulously like one of the faithful who has just been contaminated by some impurity. You remained in the water for a long time, savouring the submersion of your black thoughts, and the resurgence of your vital rhythm which regained the ascendancy and bathed you in languor. Then you started to hum one of the songs composed at the beginning of your stay in the citadel of exile and which you had sung in the court room in response to the verdict which the court President had just pronounced over your heads:

> *Tomorrow we shall return, comrades*
> *We shall return without doubt*
> *Prison shall not stop us*
> *nor its dangers.*
> *The will of the people*
> *shall not be broken . . .*

You remember the stupefaction which at that moment had paralysed the Guardians of Prosperity who had been brought in to fill up half of the room, the disarray of the judges who gathered their papers hurriedly together and literally took flight, of the emotions of the families and the lawyers who profited from the general confusion to hold you closely and to give you one last big hug before separation.

> *The epoch of the tyrants of the day*
> *is overturned*
> *and their sun is moving*
> *towards its setting.*

Then a gentle nostalgia overtakes you. Its subject is not only the past but the future. And this feeling seems the best possible definition of freedom.

"O.K. I'm going to sing something by Jara."
"Yes, do that."

Levántate y mírate las manos
Para crecer, estréchalas a tu hermano.
Juntos iremos unidos en la sangre . . .

Rise and look at your hands.
To grow, reach out towards your brother,
Together we shall go, united in our blood. . .

Awdah. Your slender voice which rises from your breast still hoarse with the sorrow it has overcome. A thin thread, without tremolos, but so powerful because it carries in its loving ardour as much as the most powerful river could carry. Your voice which in turn releases the immeasurable parting, our diaspora which as a Promised Land had only the permanence of its hopes, its faith in a human continent the size of our beautiful planet, free from plundering Templars. Releasing layer upon layer of daily irritations, the vortex of solitude or the annoyances of material life, enslavement to those tasks which one cannot refuse without appearing heretical even in the eyes of those nearest, the barren nights crossed by obscure fantasms, still-born cries against the emptiness of a body letting its undefended fruit rot at its feet, the seven-headed hatred which used to invade your heart to the point where it buried the entire universe in the same, undifferentiated malediction; the doubts which could not but catch you on your own, on this lonely voyage as unsure as that of a probe sent outside our galaxy, the wearing away caused by a dull and pitiless existence lived only at the most superficial level, the thankless mediocrity which fills up and chokes the immediate future, the drought which you believed at one time had reached to the very bottom of your soul, dried up the well-head of your emotions and your enthusiasms, blowing over our love the sirocco of uncertainty.

Awdah. Your voice pouring forth your sweetness which flows over my purified body while I am picked out by your worn fingers on the strings of the guitar.

Yo no canto por cantar
ni por tener buena voz.
Canto porque la guitarra
tiene sentido y razón . . .

I do not sing for the sake of singing
nor because I have a voice,
I sing because the guitar
is both right and true . . .

Awdah. Why have you chosen to borrow the voice of my great Chilean brother? Why do you join yourself to me across his broken fingers, his back riddled with bullets, his peaceful face resting in the bitter smile of martyrdom? Why do you plunge me into this upheaval which almost suffocates my heart? Now your image is blurred and your voice is silent. Victor is here. He is incarnated at the centre of our coming together as those who strongly love each other. We are somewhere in an unreachable spot in the heart of Chile, in the heart of Morocco, in the heart of the land of humanity. Our great brother speaks to us with the language of a clear heart, of the depths of the forests and of the pampas with its accents of genesis.

Hello, my love. Hello Victor. How do you manage

to play with those stumps better than you ever played with your fingers of rebellious faith? How is it that today I can understand your language better than the one I imbibed with my mother's milk? What shall I call the love which you have awakened in me and which is as strong as the love I bear the one who shared my trial? You are beautiful my brother. How I would have liked to have caressed your broken hands. But I am afraid of destroying everything by this incongruous gesture, afraid to shatter this moment which we have just shared together, afraid to see once again the oceans, the frontiers, the death-squads reconstitute themselves to separate us. I stop myself from moving, I refrain from all desire so that you remain here, and so that I can impregnate myself with the miracle of your voice.

Yo pregunto a los presente
si no se han puesto a pensar
que esta tierra es de nosotros
y no del que tenga mas . . .

I ask those here
if they have never thought to themselves
that this land belongs to us
and not to those who have everything . . . .

Awdah. Remember this moment. This fusion. There's no guarantee that we shall ever live again this miracle that we have created ourselves. You know very well that miracles never repeat themselves.

"Do you want me to sing something else?"

"I want you."

Away with prisons. Away with icy nights when my useless arms lay at my sides like two grass snakes abandoning themselves to the blind cycle of hibernation. Away with primordial nightmares in which I saw myself run, half of my body bloody, cut from top to bottom, in a graveyard which stretched as far as the eye could see. Away with insane visions sprung from the individual and the collective consciousness. Away with my fears as I lay chained to the Fountain of Youth. Away with my double. I offer you my fullness and my awakening. I offer you my wounds and my sorrow. I offer you the time of my memory to the furthest limits of my stewardship over the infinite. I offer you my death, to which I held out my hand the day I knew it was waiting behind my thrice-locked door. I offer you my song, a willed celebration of your hidden face, of your sweetness, the key to your power. I offer you the joy which I enjoined on you in the first torrid winter of our separation. I offer you my intact heart, my hair lifted by the wind of rediscovery. Take me. Take all these things in me. Don't stop at the parts, the fragments. Pass your hand over the scars and stitches, resolder me, rejoin me. Energise me body and soul. Then make me whole. Use me to fill the horizons and fill them with your fullness. Melt me in your crucible of generation, plunge into it my death and yours so that together we are reborn in greater clarity. Make your eyes bring us into the presence of the suns we have lost, the oceans which have been taken from us, the forests that we have been forbidden to enter while they thrust under our noses the machine-gun of

orders and the order of machine-guns. Lose me to
find me again at the heart of your delirium. Tremble
and cry beneath the hard whip of my offered power.
Whip me with your enlarged power to the extremity
of my last spasm. Let us bless the shudder of life. Let
us rise up united like this in archetypal offering.

5.

She is here on your knees. You are stroking her hair. You cannot tell the time or the place. You cannot even see her face. You do not know if she is the same wide-awake little girl who did not shed a single tear as she saw you leave that January morning with men whom she had never seen before, or whether she is the baby who had just been born and who has grown so much that she can be confused with the other when you get muddled about the chronological order of events.

She is leaning her head against you and every time you stop stroking it, she says: "More." You are in a kind of dream-space or realistic fantasy where the Little Prince ends up by becoming visible to his charmed listener and says to him: "Draw me a sheep." A child can sense your inclination at once. He knows how to get out of you your store of marvels, which allow him to furnish his childhood like a doll's house, to put on magic boots, thanks to which he can win his race with the grown-ups to find the treasure of truth.

"One day you promised to write a story for me. Tell it now."

"It may be a bit complicated."

"What do you mean? I'm not a baby any more, I'll understand. So tell it."

"You won't fall asleep?"

"That depends."

"Depends on what?"

"Obviously, on whether your story is interesting or not!"

"What makes a story interesting for you?"

"I don't know. Maybe if there's a little girl like me who does amazing things."

"And if this does not happen? If it's about a small sick boy who dreams in his bed and to whom nothing happens?"

"You're making fun of me. Go on, tell it."

The child releases herself from your embrace, puts her head on your shoulder and turns her face to you. It's not that of the elder nor the younger. It has something of both, also something of your eldest son, who had grown so much you had to look up a bit to talk to him when he came to see you on a visit.

You don't know where to begin. You rely a lot on your power of improvisation. You've just got to find an opening, and the rest will follow. You remember your mother and your paternal uncle in similar circumstances when you asked them to tell you a story. Once you had a promise from them there was a few moments' silence before the story would start. And this silence seemed interminable to you, to the extent that you were not really sure whether they were going to keep their word or not, whether they really had a new story in their heads already. Then suddenly the familiar opening words were spoken.

113

You were reassured. You abandoned yourself to the world of marvels.

Once apon a time in a country by the sea of shadows there lived a little girl called Saïda. She was no prettier, no braver, no naughtier than other little girls of her age. She had only one peculiar characteristic: she loved the sun of her land very much.

During the day she was happy. One could hear her clear laughter for ten miles around when she played with the other children. But when night fell she became sad, so sad that all the children stopped running and playing and all of them, just as sad as she was, went home.

She used to get up at dawn and open her window to look at the sunrise. And when its first rays reached out to caress her face, she had tears in her eyes, tears of joy.

At the end of every afternoon she used to run towards the sea. She would sit on a rock and look towards the horizon. She stayed there until the sun drowned in the sea. Her face would cloud over and the tears of misery which ran from her eyes were like rain from a large black cloud.

I have to say that all the inhabitants of this country used to love the sun. When they were hungry it was enough for them to bathe their faces in its light for them to feel less hungry. When they had finished their hard work and were exhausted, it was enough for them to hold out their painful limbs to the sun and they felt less tired.

Well, there was in this country a greedy ruler who

was very wealthy like all the rulers of this time who lived in the obscurity of their castles which it was forbidden to go near.

It was two years since it had last rained. A great drought had come. The fields no longer gave a harvest. The animals were dying of thirst and hunger. In addition the ruler was angry because the people had no money to pay their taxes. He tried to think of a scheme to get money into his treasury, which had become almost empty. At that moment he was told that a great foreign magician wanted to meet him.

"Let him come in," said the ruler.

The great magician came in. He came from across the sea of shadows. He had heard people talking about the drought which had blighted the country and about the anger of its ruler.

"Sir," he said, "I have a solution to your problems."

"What's that?" asked the ruler, who was very interested.

"Have you considered making use of your most valuable asset, your Excellency?"

"And what is that, magician?"

"Look, Excellency, these rays which come through the window of the room, this sun which disappears only to reappear, warmer and more powerful. You have there an incalculable fortune."

"What are you suggesting, then?" asked the ruler.

"Make a profit out of it, Excellency. You must know that on the other side of the sea of shadows there are countries where the sun seldom appears. If you succeed, in the way that I am thinking of, in exploiting yours, you can sell it to them in the way that one sells the copper, the silver and the coal that one gets out of the earth. Your fortune will be assured by this forever, because the sun, unlike copper, silver or coal, is inexhaustible."

"Your idea is brilliant!" exclaimed the ruler. "I give you *carte blanche* and you shall have as many men as you require. And if you succeed in your undertaking I shall give you the hand of my daughter. (What am I saying? thought the ruler to himself, as he got a bit confused.) Well, let's say I will concede to you half of my profits."

"You can rely on me, Excellency."

"To work then!" ordered the ruler.

The great magician went to work. He ordered the ruler's workmen to build a large mobile tower. Some weeks later the tower was ready, reaching up to the sky. It was so high that wherever you went in the country you could still see it. The tower was like a crane with a huge trunk at the end. It followed the sun in its trajectory from the moment it appeared on rising to the moment it disappeared on setting. It greedily swallowed the rays which went down into its belly where a factory had been set up. There millions and millions of bottles were filled with the sun's rays. The bottles were then loaded onto big boats which set off for the other side of the sea of shadows and which returned months later, full of gold and of all kinds of goods that the ruler had asked for.

After a few weeks the sun began to shine less. The inhabitants of the country realised that it did not console them for their hunger and their pains as it had done before. They well understood that the great magician was responsible for that. But they were afraid to speak out because the ruler had his spies

everywhere and they used to report all criticisms to him.

From the very first days that the tower began to be built Saïda had changed. She no longer played with other children the same age as herself. Her clear laughter could no longer be heard for ten miles around. Every afternoon she could be seen going towards the sea, sitting on a rock facing the horizon and looking at her dear friend before he disappeared. It might almost be said that Saïda and the sun were talking to one another.

"Don't be unhappy, my sweet little friend," the sun would say.

"How can I not be unhappy when the tower of the great magician is drinking your blood day by day? Look how pale you have become. Soon you will have no more blood."

"Don't worry my little friend, you know very well that suns do not die, because they live also in the hearts of human beings, above all in the hearts of small children like yourself who enquire after them each day, follow them both asleep and awake, in their rising and their setting."

"But this tower, don't you feel its claws in your flesh? Doesn't it take your blood?"

"Yes, it's true. I feel the damage it's doing to me. But by myself, I have no head and no arms. It's only when I enter into the head and the arms of men that I have a body which can act and get rid of these claws which pierce my flesh."

"Well then, I can do something for you."

"Yes, you can if you are able to become the body that I spoke of."

"I don't really understand. But I shall do something."

"Think carefully, my sweet little friend. Beware of the ruler and his spies."

"Don't worry. I'm only a little girl. No one will take any notice of me."

Saïda did not cry any more. She did not cry and she did not laugh. When she went out into the street she walked with a firm step. Her face had taken on the serious look of an adult. But what no one knew was that Saïda left home every day a little before dawn. She evaded the eye of the watchmen at the factory and went into the belly of the tower. She had a small bag of sand hidden under her dress and she scattered it over the cog-wheels of the great machine. In this way, every night, another little bag until the day when the men in charge of the machine arrived at dawn, tried to get it going as usual, but failed. The ruler was told immediately and he ordered that the magician be dragged from his bed. When he arrived on the spot he shouted:

"It's sabotage!"

"It's sabotage!" the men chorused in response.

"Sabotage!" cried the angry ruler. "Find out who's responsible. And make sure everything is working again before sunset!"

The ruler's spies spread out through the country. Everyone was questioned. At the end of the day, they got together to analyse the results of their enquiry. Their information was very poor. They despaired of presenting themselves empty-handed before the ruler and of incurring some terrible punishment, when, just before sunset, a former spy came and asked to talk to them. They let him in.

118

"What have you to tell us?" asked the chief spy.

"I think I know who caused the sabotage. You see, I live beside the factory. I wake up each day before dawn to pray. I always leave my bedroom window open. Well, two or three times I have seen a little girl slip through the door of the factory. I thought she was the daughter of one of the watchmen. But now I have my suspicions."

"Tell us what she's like."

The retired spy gave Saïda's description. They came to get her when she was by the sea, sitting on a rock, telling something to the sun who was listening with a serious air.

In spite of her age, the ruler ordered that she should be locked up in a small dark room where the sun never shone. She stayed there for three months, sad that she could no longer go and meet her friend and sad that she could not greet him each morning. One day she had an idea. She took a safety pin which she had used to fasten her apron where she had lost a button and began to scratch the wall of her room. Day after day, she scratched at the same place to make a hole in the wall. She continued to dig and dig, day and night, until the safety pin reached the other side of the wall. She enlarged the hole so that a pale ray of sun could get into her room. Saïda greeted him with a great cry of joy. She caressed him, let him caress her and told him everything she was thinking.

But her happiness didn't last long. The next day a spy came into her room and found the hole in the wall. He immediately ordered it to be filled in. Saïda could not bear this unhappiness. She decided not to eat any more if they would not let her have her sunshine. The spies tried in vain to persuade her. They brought her toys, each one more beautiful than the last, cakes, each one more delicious than the last. Nothing worked. The spies could not disguise their amazement at the stubbornness of this little girl who claimed her sun in the face of death.

The news finally spread to the four corners of the country by the side of the sea of shadows. Little by little, tongues were loosened. People became less and less afraid that their protests would reach the ears of the ruler. They even took their defiance to the extent of marching up to the giant tower and raising their fists towards its trunk in a threatening way. Even when the spies drove them away, they came back the next day and looked menacingly at the trunk of the tower.

Saïda died one day at dawn, without ever having touched the toys or the cakes which filled her room.

But when the men in charge of the machine arrived at dawn and tried to get it going as usual, they could not.

Again, they immediately told the ruler who ordered that the magician be dragged out of his bed. He arrived on the spot and after examining the machine cried:

"Another sabotage!"

"Another sabotage!" the men chorused in response.

"Another sabotage!" cried the angry ruler. And he gave orders that they should find out who was guilty.

The spies now knew where to find the guilty. They had no need even to question people. They went to the seaside, close to the rock where Saïda used to sit and talk to the sun. There they found not one but dozens of children. But before taking them away they were struck by what the children were looking at. On the horizon there was not just one sun, as usual at sunset. There were two. The everyday sun and, alongside it, almost touching it, a sun which was very small but still visible even to the naked eye. The small sun slowly drew closer to the large one, then touched it and finally blended into it. Then the single sun became bigger and redder and after a long time it finally plunged into the sea.

The spies picked out three children and took them away. The next day they came and took three more children. And so, each day. But every day three more children replaced those who had disappeared. Each day three more children joined the others to see the coming together of the small sun and the large one which got bigger and redder than an ordinary sun.

"That's it."

"That's it, it's finished?"

"How did you like it?"

"It was not very cheerful. Was it true?"

"Yes, there are true things in it and also imaginary things. Without that, there wouldn't be any stories."

"And Saïda, did she exist?"

"Of course. It might even have been you, a little bit now, a lot one day, who knows?"

"I would not like to die of hunger. But I would like to be this little sun which made the large one bigger."

"That's the root of the problem, my little sardine, pretty little ladybird."

"Tell me another."

"Don't be greedy, my little gazelle. You have to go to bed now."

You had woken up early this morning. Was this a prison habit or because you knew that you, your wife and yourself, had to go to collect the children from the airport? Sitting on your bed you had given yourself over to these musings which never ceased to surprise you. How were stories born in the imagination of men, what part is played by individual creativity and what part by collective re-creation, how was this symbolic heritage transmitted from one people to another, how did they create this melting pot where they elaborated archetypes characteristic of a certain time or place but which ended up by becoming universal?

You get up and go to the children's rooms. You go first to the bedroom of your eldest child. It felt humid because of the damp which had made large stains at the corners of the walls and on the ceiling. The walls are practically bare except for a poster stuck over the bed which showed a space walk, some reproductions of animals and flowers, a beautiful picture of Mayakovsky with his head shaved and holding a black dog in his arms.

The room is well laid out. There are some shelves with a collection of rocks. Each rock carries a label with its common name, its scientific name and the place where it was collected. A small library is meticulously arranged, reading books for adolescents, school text-books, scientific works and magazines, tourist brouchures and maps. On the desk there is another set of shelves carrying a variety of objects: toys, a few little tarnished figures some of which go back to the earliest days of childhood (you recognise a soft, spotted dog, a little straw Mexican figure with a large hat), a radio set with all its insides showing, which is apparently used for do-it-yourself or some experiment, a beginner's microscope, a barometer, stuff for stamp-collecting.

You are careful not to disturb anything. You are satisfied to gaze at this multifaceted mirror which gives you back the scattered image of the child you left when he was seven years old. Now he is nearly sixteen. A young man whose ideas, temperament and character were forged in torment. In spite of all the efforts you had made during the course of those long years to remain available to him, attached to his life, to make him familiar with yours, dedramatise it and make it comprehensible to him in its actual implications, you knew very well then and you know even better today that you were becoming slowly estranged from each other. Not in the sense of a lack of understanding, indifference, the loss of mutual feeling, let alone hostility. You were certain it was not a matter of that. What was bound to happen, and to counter which you could do nothing, was the growth of two parallel lines between which there could certainly be some osmosis but also an imperviousness as time passed: the daily sufferings and discourses which forge everyone and fashion the unique experience of each individual, the shadowy areas, reactions which are unpredictable to others but not for oneself, not to mention the likes and dislikes, the pleasing and the disgusting, what opens the heart towards another and what shuts it off. This life experience is as intractable as facts. You know now that you have to recapture lost time, at least in so far

123

as you can recapture it, that it is the new life which will be a determining factor, but you also know that you are not starting from scratch. In spite of everything, the shared suffering has made you similar to a degree which is unusual in ordinary life. It has made of you one body which is both united and disparate. Like Siamese twins who have been maladroitly separated by an absent-minded surgeon, you reacted in the same way when threatened, you had the same anxious care for one another and you had a sixth sense, that of fraternity.

You remember with affection the letters and poems which your son used to write to you, above all during the early years. You found them wonderful in their surrealistic freshness or solemn seriousness. A pure and naked cry informed them. You read in them the most overwhelming denunciation of the circumstances which had created you and of the system which produced and reproduced them. Thanks to these letters, you had discovered that poetry and the passion for life was ageless and that children could be not only precursors but also originators. And then you had begun to listen seriously to this new human species.

You leave the room and open your daughters': the middle and the youngest of your children. It's dark in here but you can gradually make out the furniture and the other things it is filled with: wooden bunk-beds, a desk and chair, a smaller desk with a stool, a large wall cupboard with a mirror in the middle, a set of shelves bending under the weight of books and magazines heaped together, soft toys and animals, boxes of games. The atmosphere of disorder makes you daring. You open the desk drawer which you assume must belong to the youngest. You smile at the spectacle of this pharmacopoeia, the flavour of which only the genius of a Balzac could attempt to capture. You notice a black plastic case. You open it with a gesture of tender curiosity. There are two identical photos in it, yours taken at a time when you still wore a tie and when your beard was only a narrow strip, that of Saïda, the one which had circulated in prison and which had made her more familiar to you: a young woman with a light complexion, with fine features and whose wondering gaze gave her eyes the beauty peculiar to short-sighted people when they take off their spectacles.* You return the case to the drawer and push it shut. You have a slight feeling of remorse. That of having intruded without permission into a sanctuary of feeling so fragile that any word, any abrupt gesture could hurt it.

"What are you doing here?"

Your wife is leaning on the door. She must have woken up when she suddenly felt your empty place in the bed.

"I'm behaving a bit like those pre-Islamic poets who returned to contemplate the remains of the camp where they had first encountered the Beloved."

"And what remains were you looking for here?"

"That of the camp of our pre-history. Us two, the children. The traces left by time which has put here all those things which have become so many signs of our separation. I was making myself familiar with the new walls I have to scale in order truly to return from exile."

* Saïda Muebbhi, a Moroccan activist, was imprisoned in 1976 and died, aged 25, in 1977, while on hunger strike.

"You also have to help the children to scale their own walls, so that they can recover not a miraculous father but just a father plain and simple."

"Will I ever be a good father?"

"That's not the problem. It's enough that you are not one they cannot understand."

"You're right. At one time I rarely thought about them as individuals. I simply placed them in the category of disinherited children. Even if I credited them with a higher expectation of life than the majority of others, even if I saw them better fed and better dressed than the others, my contacts with them were as abstract as other contacts I had with reality. Paradoxically, prison forced me to rediscover them. In a way I had not attended to before, as individuals, particular beings, with particular needs, small personalities which were not copied from any model or pattern. And this was a great discovery. Far from blurring the dialectic of the general and the particular, it allowed me to distinguish it better. Childhood was no more a haze, a miniature reproduction of the drama which was being played but on a larger scale on the social scene. I was opening my eyes to flesh and blood children. I followed the path of their injuries, I sensed the unbearable suffering in their eyes, I read there the saga of all our deprivations. They had finally given to me the key to their city. I had entered it. And I began to observe and to study it. Believe me, I learned a lot . . . ."

You suddenly stop speaking. You read on your wife's face a mixed expression. You go out of the room and close the door.

"O.K.," you say. "We'll still have to go into all that. Ready?"

"Let's go. We have just enough time to get to the airport."

The plane comes to a halt. You can hardly believe that this steel mastodon manages to get off the ground, cut its way through the sky, fly over seas and mountains, leap from one continent to another, carrying in its belly carefree passengers who remain sunk in their seats, taking no notice of anything, quietly reading their papers or hungrily eating the meal served to them. Like pre-historic man who has emerged from the forgotten continent of his jungle, you are still fascinated by this grandiose machinery, only half believing that it could be the work of the simple ingenuity of man. But around you, on the airport terrace, you realise that no one is excited. People are confidently waiting for the passengers' arrival. Even babes-in-arms smile and point to the machine as if it were a nice toy in a shop window.

The door of the aircraft opens. But instead of the mobile stairs there is a large enclosure mounted on a truck which goes towards the plane and is fastened over the door. You will therefore not have the customary wave from a distance. You have to go back to the waiting room.

You go down. You stand in front of the arrivals hall. You wait. All around people are leaving and arriving. You don't know why but you read on their faces a certain self-satisfaction. As if to take a plane conferred a certain social status, a superiority over those who could not cross frontiers and atmospheres and had to content themselves with getting on a bus or hailing a taxi.

The passengers start to emerge and pass customs. Your heart is beating madly. You smoke nervously.

"There they are!" your wife shouts.

"Where?"

"There, behind that group of women."

You can't see their heads. It's a smile which you just spot, then hands are waved in your direction. You wave your hand in turn, send them a smile. But they soon turn their backs and go to look for their luggage and present themselves at customs. They look at you again, weighed down with bags, they smile at you while waving. A single smile, a single hand, a body of intoxicating fluidity comes closer and closer and finally encloses you in the wonder of held-back tears, of the kiss with a thousand flavours of joy.

After the Journey
this jumble of roots
this passion for identity
In this way the ordeal armed me
against the blind thrusts of History
I remount the curve of evil times
to unearth my anchored memory
I prefigure my death
among my familiars
I prepare myself for the solemn erosion
which will make me germinate in the earth.

6

Fes. It's well and truly a pilgrimage to your well-springs that you wanted. You allow this thought without its drawing the least protest from you. A lot of terms you've been using lately have lost their single meanings. You have shattered the monopoly of appropriation. They have made their way through you to re-emerge marked by your own hells and paradises, charged with a new sap which reaches them from the network of roots which you have woven in order to bind together words and their most vital energy. It is then really a pilgrimage: a quest and its objective, a circumvolution around certain places where memory is reborn from ashes, a secret prayer that windows will open in the heart, oxygenating smell, hearing, sight, sweeping away the cobwebs of forgetting, bringing down the barricades.

This pilgrimage which you have undertaken so often in imagination. Ever since the day when your wife had brought you the news.

She had been so gentle and loving that afternoon during the visit. You had talked about the court trial which had just ended.

"You know, I was expecting ten years. And I got them," you had said jokingly.

"Me too, that's what I was expecting."

The waiting room was particularly noisy. Prisoners and visitors were still in a state of shock. They needed to talk in order to get used to a new situation, organise a new life, give each other courage. The voice of one woman could be heard above the tumult. She was the mother of one of your comrades. A gigantic peasant woman who was holding forth in Berber and showering curses over the heads of those who had just sentenced her son, right under the bewildered and powerless eyes of the warders. She was beating with her fists on the grill. The shock waves spread. The grill was bumping the noses and the foreheads of those visitors who were straining so that they could see the prisoners better in the bad light of the visiting room.

You were far from unhappy that day. Your wife was reminding you of some of the more grotesque aspects of the trial. Those young policemen armed with old guns who were placed near the exit at the end of the room and whose only job was to present arms when the Court rose. The happy-go-lucky fellows who were rather unaware of the seriousness of the charges against them and who never missed a chance to ridicule them. The old lawyer who read a whole series of *Crapouillot* under the table while following the day's proceedings with half an ear but who, when his turn came round, had worked up an outrageous plea which finally united in one outburst of hilarity the accused, the families, police and judges. He had managed therefore to drown in an abrasive surge of laughter the specious charges made by the prosecution.

"What was the joke he told and which caused so much laughter?"

"Oh yes. He compared our trial to the story of the old Fassi woman. A widow who lived all alone in a large house and who almost never went out. This all happened well before the Protectorate, when *harka* levies were raised by the Sultanate to try and pacify the countryside. Fes was mobilised. Agents were going from house to house to register new recruits or to collect money. The agents finally arrived at the home of this widow, Kirana. They explained to her what it was all about and called on her to support the *harka* and fulfil her obligations. And so she declared: 'Well, I can see from here what kind of *harka* it's going to be if Kirana is called upon to take part in it!' "

The shaft of humour was double-edged. But it seemed essentially to show that it was not volleys of tracts and brochures that could overthrow a government as the prosecution liked to claim.

You remembered the character of another lawyer. He was conducting the defence of your comrades who were accused of having thrown bombs at the quarters of the police force. The lawyer improvised in the style of an actor from Jamaâ Lafna Square in order to mime the supposed deeds of sabotage. He tossed an imaginary bag full of Molotov cocktails over his shoulder and began to walk up and down the room like a Haddaoui intoning: "Glory to you, prophet of God!" From time to time he took an imaginary bottle out of his bag, threw it, waited for it to land and then mimicked the noise of a badly-made device that failed to explode: Tchch! Tchchch!

"There you are, Mr President, it is actions like those

132

that my client is supposed to have carried out. Judge for yourself the seriousness of the charge."

Another funny incident. When a third lawyer asked permission to put before the court the ideas of the accused. He held in his hands a paperback he had obviously just bought. One of those books like *Do It Yourself* or *How to Feed your Cat*, and which was probably called *All You Need to Know about Marxism*. He launched himself into a faltering explanation of the idea of socialism from Plato to Mao Tse-Tung, passing through primitive socialism and putting into the same bag the socialisation of the means of production and the holding of women in common. He was unable to stop himself despite loud protests and jeers from all around, from the benches of the accused as well as from the judges.

"I implore you," the President finally interrupted him. "Enough, sir, we have understood."

You also reflected on the entertaining behaviour of certain of the accused under cross-examination. One of them made you laugh when in reply to a question put to him by the President, he simply doubled up and repeated:

"Mr President, my back, my back hurts. They beat me!"

"Do you know X?"

"My back, Mr President."

"When and where did you meet Y for the first time?"

"They beat me, Mr President. My back."

"Go back to your seat," the President finally said, having lost the battle.

The warders had begun to clink their keys against the bars which separated you, and to knock on the door at the entrance to the visiting room. You had to hurry up and end the visit. You noticed your wife hesitate for a moment. Then her eyes filled with tears, and you knew by a slight tremor and pursing of her lips that something was wrong. She turned her head away, unable to stand your questioning look.

"What's the matter?"

"You know, I had something to tell you. I'm sorry I didn't do it sooner."

"What is it?"

"Your mother is dead."

"When?"

"The twenty-seventh of July."

"How did she die?"

"You know she already had high blood pressure. Then she became sort of anorexic. For some weeks she had refused to eat."

"Why didn't you tell me about it when it happened?"

"Your family begged me not to, to wait until the trial ended."

"And did you think that it could have changed anything in my behaviour, had some effect on my morale?"

"No, you know that. But I had promised. Do you forgive me?"

"Yes, of course."

The warders brutally pulled the curtain. You had scarcely time to see a tear run down your wife's face. Then nothing. The curtain hid everything. Your eyes were dry.

"Good-bye," your wife was still saying on the other side of the curtain.

"Good-bye. Don't worry," you said finally.

You took your basket and went out of the visiting room. In the exercise yard the light was blinding. Your eyes were still dry. A feeling of emptiness in your brain and in your heart. A kind of irritation. As if you had not had and could not have the appropriate reaction. It was true, you had learned not to dramatise any more. From the beginning of the ordeal you had collected and received so many hard knocks. In its recurrence death no longer had the bitter taste of the destructive unknown. It had become familiar, an ordinary actor in the collective drama.

You had gone back to your cell. On the way friends had asked if you had any news. You told them the week's news. As on previous occasions. Nothing in your voice or in your manner had given you away. You were ashamed of their hearing this particular news just like that, all of a sudden. It would be a bolt from the blue. News like this was not part and parcel of the joint focus of interest in the collective life. It did not fall under one of the relevant headings like arrests, executions, official pronouncements, the internal and external changes in the lives of political organisations, their deals with the powers that be or their petty quarrels, the solidarity campaigns with prisoners in other countries, information about economics, the mass struggle of workers, peasants, students and school children, the responses of commercial and agricultural bodies, the new stories which circulated about such and such a well-known person, the rumours broadcast by Radio Medina about a possible ministerial shuffle, the disgrace of one and the reappearance on the political scene of another, about an act of clemency which might take place on the occasion of a religious or national feast. No, this news arose from private life. It had no place under the relevant headings and could have no re-percussions whatsoever on them.

You returned to your cell with two others. At that time you were three to a cell. You had taken out the food brought by your families. You had eaten while chatting about the week's events. After drinking tea, each one had resumed his place. Each of your comrades had got a book out and had begun to read. Unlike other occasions you did not begin to write a letter to your wife to talk about the visit and to prolong the state of grace of your meeting. You lay down. You unfolded a blanket. You used it to cover your whole body, even your head. Then you had opened your eyes in the darkness. You stayed like that for a long time, not moving, until you began to feel a sensation of suffocation rising from your stomach, an irritation in your throat before the tears began to flow fast without your being able to do anything about it. Quite a bit later – you must certainly have sobbed – you felt a hand placed on your head. A comrade was calling you. You lifted the blanket.

"What's the matter with you," he asked. "Are you ill?"

"Yes . . . No. It's nothing. Some bad news."

"What is it?"

"My mother is dead."

At these words the other left his place and came up

136

to you. He took your hand while the other continued to stroke your head absent-mindedly. None of the three of you knew what to say. Silence filled the cell until the moment when the warder came round to put out the light. You remained like that in the darkness. Then one of your friends murmured in a quiet warm voice in your direction:

"Courage, comrade, courage!"

"Thank you, comrade. I'll be O.K.," you had replied.

Your friends returned to their places. You opened your eyes again in the darkness of the cell which had now become total. Silence reigned, broken from time to time by the noise the rats made scratching the bottom of the bucket which you had filled with water to make it heavy and which you placed over the hole of the w.c. to protect yourselves against these nocturnal pests. The rats knocked against the bucket, got mad, moved it a bit without being able to overturn it. They finally left, hoping to find a way out somewhere else if some less farsighted comrade had forgotten to put his bucket there as he ought to or, absent-mindedly, had put it there but forgotten to fill it with water.

You stared into the darkness. You were looking for something. Yes, you were trying to recover the colour of your mother's eyes. She had eyes of a particular greenish-blue, more green than blue, like marjoram when it is still fresh. But those colours remained at the level of abstractions. You could not manage to blend them to restore the true colour and consequently the particular clarity of her look, this clarity which might have allowed you from now on to call it up in her absence and to give her the voice which she had never had, and which she should have had, in life.

You can't tell how you fell asleep. A knock-out blow to the head which immediately plunged you into the vortex of a dream.

The scene opens on the small house of 'Ayn Al Khayl where you first saw the light of day and where you spent the first days of your childhood. All the neighbourhood is gathered to help at the double ceremony. The family is all there. But this is no longer the small clan whose ranks were scattered more than thirty years ago that you see again. It's a real tribe which parades before you, nephews and nieces, children of cousins, husbands and wives of all that progeniture. Faces you cannot put a name to but who all have what one might call a familiar air. You are there, in the middle of the crowd, in the splendid clothes of the newly circumcised. You are wearing a green embroidered tarbouch on your head, with a kaftan and babouches of the same colour with the same embroidery. You are enthroned on a chair of painted wood. You pay no more attention to the pain which radiates out from your new scar because there's so much going on. Responding to the sounds of the *ghaïtas* and the wild beatings of the tambours, there are the piercing cries of the chorus of wailing women. All around you faces are impassive. They express neither sorrow nor joy. You look in vain for your father in the midst of the crowd. You can't find him. The wailing women suddenly appear. They come out of your parents' bedroom. But instead of uttering cries, they begin to let out youyous and to recite propitiatory formulas that are only pronounced on

138

happy occasions. They are bearing on their shoulders a mortuary slab on which a corpse is stretched out. They parade around a central courtyard of the house and then put down their burden. Their youyous rise up more beautifully. The *ghaïtas* bawl out amid the mad beating of the tambours. Your mother is stretched out on the slab, rigid but with a strange beauty. Made-up, wearing her bridal dress, she looks as if she has just closed her eyes like any bride during the wedding ceremony. Relatives and neighbours come closer and take out of their pockets bank notes which they wave around ostentatiously before slipping them into the embroidered golden waist-band, four fingers wide, around your mother's waist. Each gift provokes more youyous. Finally your father emerges from the crowd. He is crying. You notice he is the only one who is crying. He goes up to your mother, takes the bank notes and gives them to the woman who appears to be the chief mourner. At the same time the women mourners lift up the slab and go towards the door of the house. Once there they try unsuccessfully to pass through it but the door is too narrow. They try in every possible way. Nothing works. In a final attempt, they lift the slab up as if it were a wheelbarrow. The body slips and is on the point of tipping out onto the steep road. You feel your heart beating wildly. You are suffocating. Your body does not obey you any more. It's getting heavier and heavier as if it's being crushed by a gigantic press. You want to cry out and call for help but you can't speak any more. You know that you simply must call out to free yourself from being crushed and to recover the use of your limbs. You struggle with yourself for a long time before you find sufficient energy to release your cry. You start off with a low moaning which you increase bit by bit in intensity until the moment when you are sure that you can make the leap. You then force out the vital cry for deliverance. You know just at that moment someone will come to waken you.

"Are you ill? Shall I call the warder?"

"No, it's not worth it. I was suffocating. I'm all right now."

"Do you want a drink?"

"Yes, please."

Your comrade goes to the tap in the darkness. You take the water. You drink and lie down again.

"You're sure you're O.K.?"

"Yes, I feel better."

Bit by bit, you get your breath back. Your heartbeat recovers its normal rhythm. You lie on your back so that you can embrace night's blackness more easily. You think about your dream. You don't try to decipher it. You look at it as a work of art by the double who lives in your body, ceaselessly weaves the weft of the dark places of your fears and your obsessions. Then a single idea arises from the labyrinth of your terror, a promise. Yes, you promise that the first thing that you will do, if one day you should be free, is to take yourself to the grave of your mother in Fes.

Fes. Which you are looking at now. You only had to take in the view of this city and your memory underwent a metamorphosis. It is no longer the pool lying still behind your eyes and whose surface you disturb as if throwing pebbles when you want to free the waves of recollection. It has suddenly embodied itself in this town which stretches at your feet like a lascivious virgin.

Your gaze only skims over the surface of the chequered terraces, the arches sweeping or broken by domes, the bare towers of the minarets, the foliage which swarms like hidden thickets of fluff growing out of nubile armpits, the bare hills, like rounded breasts, swelled by the insistent caress of the dying sun. You soon sense a kind of inhalation. And it's true that the town breathes. Its breath is a diffuse noise made up of tinklings and rustlings whose sonorous echo you do not hear but which rises in waves like small, vaporous clouds, reddish-violet, from the panting dust of the city. You soon feel the pulse of the scattered heart which beats out an old tune with an Andalusian accent. You soon sense the spreading of roots which reach out and wrap themselves around your limbs, plunge themselves into your body, and the history of the place rolls over you with a fullness which irons out ambiguity, doubt and the barrier of your successive exiles.

It's then that you are struck by the beauty of this town. A beauty that's not inscribed on its monuments and buildings, the vault of the sky, the tops of the trees or the curve of the hills, but exists more in the harmony between all those elements and man, men, man-as-witness as well as men-as-actors. You find there one of the secrets of its beauty. This town was not conceived of solely in terms of the normal functions of a city – professions, exchange of goods and ideas, centre of power, accumulation and redistribution of wealth. It was conceived of also as

141

something to be looked at. It appears to you in its function of a fresco which reflected the sensitivity and thought of its artisans, their harmony with nature and the world, the cry of their needs, of their torments and the pains which they have never tried to hide. You are no longer surprised by the capacity of this town to speak of itself by simply revealing itself to the gaze of any unmercenary traveller, of every pilgrim after truth. You feel very happy about this discovery. You are reassured. Your fascination has nothing to do with the spirit of preserving the past or a childish attachment to the soil. It's the powerful enigma of this city which draws you to it. And so the sphinx began to reveal its secrets. You had no longer any need to feel ashamed of your feelings of wonder.

Fes. Whose veil you now raise. So that the face of your pre-history might be revealed to you. You move forward in the surging body of your memory. You follow the tiny streets leading to the centre of the medina, where you had arranged to meet your father. It's he who will be your guide in the fulfilment of your promise. You instinctively find your way through this labyrinth whose most obscure corner used to be familiar to you. You walk slowly so as not to miss the smallest detail. Each cul-de-sac, archway, gutter, public fountain, entrance to the public bath, doorway to the Koranic school or *medersa* are the signs which now begin to glitter in the haze, descend from the pedestal of the forgotten and come to rejoin with your emotion. You no longer feel as if you are walking, but sailing along a river which crosses a city half-eaten by jungle but which is not yet dead. You glide slowly on the current, you abandon yourself to the enchantment of this voyage to your own extremities, to the end of your lost dreams, to the end of your scattered heart and of your capacities to be moved.

You enter the square with the Nejjarine fountain.

At first your gaze seems to fall on a picture postcard. But gradually as you draw nearer, another fountain takes its place. The water once again runs from its copper taps. Its arabesques are fixed one moment and then suddenly slacken and accompany in dance the secret song of the water. The square takes on its former dimensions. On the left the *fondouk* which served as the commissariat in the time of the Protectorate. On the right, the market belonging to the guild of woodworkers, which gave its name to the square. Further to the right, the market belonging to the guild of saddlers, where your father works.

You still have not finished symbolically deciphering the postcard which had met your puzzled gaze when you hear behind you your father's voice.

"You are here?"

"Yes."

"Come on then. A lot of people want to greet you."

You turn round ready to walk at his side but he's already in front of you. He walks with the same jerky steps by which you have always recognised him.

Your reunion had taken place the evening before. When you entered the house and your eyes met, he had departed from his usual custom and got up to greet you. Through force of habit he offered you his right hand, then changing his mind, he withdrew it. For a few seconds you were seized with doubt. Just for once you should have overcome your revulsion against this kind of homage, made an abstraction of the symbol it represented, mimicked the custom without paying any attention to its immediate or more distant implications. You should have been able to take his hand and lift it to your lips. You are well aware that in this precise situation, such an act could not diminish you at all, damage your dignity or be interpreted as a renunciation of the moral code you had created for yourself. But there was nothing to be done. You could not give in to the arbitrary nature of this ceremony. You remained convinced that it was only a travesty of the kind of individual respect and tenderness which you bore for the author of your life. Your father's smile rescued you. His face expressed such a childlike joy that you hurriedly pressed against yourself the head and chest of the old man who began to speak in a voice trembling on the verge of tears:

"God bless you my son. May God bless you. Let us thank Him for having brought you back safe and sound."

You pressed him against you even harder, kissed him on the cheeks while slapping his back. You had the feeling that you were pressing your own child against yourself. And you immediately forgot the old story of kissing hands.

Sekkatine market. Your head like a kaleidoscope. The images whirl. Grenada where you and your wife had discovered a street with this name: Zacatin. The complexity of your roots. Then yourself as a child, coming here to do the shopping, to have your hair cut at the barber's, whose shop was opposite your father's, to take part in the auctions which took place in the afternoon, watching your father work, buying or selling, as he initiated you, while pretending to take no notice, into the coded language that artisans and merchants here used so that they would not be understood by children or strangers in the market – customers, coming for the most part from the countryside, travelling merchants who came to stock up on goods which they resold in the rural markets. You had managed to understand the words used to suggest women, children, good or bad merchandise, cheap or dear. But there were others whose obscenity or gravity you sensed but which you had never succeeded in deciphering.

You have hardly looked at the actual market you are crossing. It is almost empty. Half the shops are closed. In the ones which are open there are no more skilled saddlers. You no longer find those humble dignitaries enveloped in their robes whom you had to greet respectfully as you passed. Strangers, mostly young, have replaced them. They are involved in new activities which have nothing to do with saddle-making.

It's only when you reach the end of the market that you recognise some of the older shops. Your father stops in front of one of them and you catch up.

"Here he is," your father says with a triumphant air, to a thick-set man with a reddish complexion who is in the middle of the shop.

You recognise your eldest uncle. At his side, another man, small, almost a dwarf. The youngest of your paternal uncles. The one whom all the family call Touissa (small cup) probably because he used to take a few too many before becoming deaf and wiser with age. He's the same uncle who had been the Homer of your childhood, the fertiliser of your imagination. The same one who had revealed to you the fantastic treasure of the Thousand and One Nights, the stories of Sif Ben Di Yazan and of Hamza Al Bahlawane.

Hugs. Formulas of welcome and compassion.

"For the sake of God, my son."

"The believer is exposed to evil."

"Let us thank God for bringing you back safe and sound."

You reply as best you can. You borrow from the only inventory of thanks and gratitude that will be accepted here. This is neither the time nor the place for iconoclasm, to purge the language of its burden of beliefs.

Your Uncle Touissa comes down from the shop. He presses himself against you. His deafness has distanced him from spoken language. He is happy to pat your hand while giving a throaty chuckle. And each time that you respond to his pressure or throw out a word in his direction, his smile becomes more beautiful, like an irresistible fit of coughing. Other people come down from the nearby shops. Come to greet you. Formulas of welcome, of compassion. Your father introduces them.

"You remember so-and-so?"

"Yes, yes, of course."

"And here's so-and-so. He has continued throughout all these years to pray for your release."

You look over these polished faces, engraved with lines, expressing the tranquil outlook which must be that of people surprised by an avalanche, whose intact bodies are recovered centuries later. You feel as if you have opened a book at the chapter about floods. You find it hard at first to understand what they are saying to you, these patriarchs who talk with the characteristics of old Fassi stock and whose sonorous accents are weakened by their tendency to diminish the role of the larynx and vocal cords. Your eldest uncle sends someone to fetch tea from the café in the market. The tea arrives. You drink it while one of those there comments on your ordeal and supports what he says with quotations from the Koran and by citing similar experiences undergone by the prophets. The listeners are moved, serious. You know that those present are experiencing a moment of heightened feeling. You end up by sharing this feeling keenly in a human way, abolishing barriers of age, of time, religious formulas invoking the sole benefactor. You participate in their simple happiness.

"We have to go now," your father says.

"Where?" asks your eldest uncle.

"He wants to go and see his mother's grave."

Formulas of blessing all round. More embraces. Your father has already headed off with the same jerky step. You follow him.

At the gateway to the market you notice a porter sitting on a step, with a sack of jute and a knotted cord thrown over his shoulders. You remember that the porters in the market used to come from a tribe in the region. You ask about it.

"Are they still from Oulad Sidi Aïssa, those who work here?"

"Yes! But there are no more than two or three now."

You cut across the potter's market.

"Let's go through here," you suggest to your father.

"We'll be going a long way round," he tells you.

"It doesn't matter. I would like to see Sidi Frej Square again."

You enter it. Access is through a covered doorway. From one end to the other there are mortuary slabs leaning against the wall. A few undertakers are sitting there, squatting. Faces of strangers who do not look at you as you pass. When you used to come here before with your father, you unfailingly witnessed a scene which always repeated itself in the same terms. One of the undertakers, an old friend of your father, would exchange a conspiratorial smile with him before calling out:

"Welcome, *Haj.* "

"Keep your welcome for yourself and chase the flies."

"God is generous, *Haj,* He provides for all his creatures."

"I hope He won't be providing for you," your father concludes, amidst general hilarity.

Like all childhood places that are seen again with the eyes of an adult, Sidi Frej Square seems to you to look so much smaller. Only the giant plane tree which stands in the middle and whose branches cover the sky, has retained its true proportions. Under its tutelary wing the liveliness of this place unfolds itself in an atmosphere of spontaneity, of light and shade. The cabbalistic exchanges among sellers of henna, ghassoul and juniper and their customers seem like a sort of whispering. On the left, close to the fountain, the great public weighing scales are still

148

there. Fossil or symbol?

Your father walks with the same lively step. You are happy in this multitude of images.

You leave the square, cut through the dense crowd of the Attarine market and go towards 'Aïn Al Khayl district: the kingdom of your childhood and the setting of the house where you were born. The little streets become darker and narrower. You find it difficult to believe that this labyrinth could have been the setting for your games and your races and that it would have represented to you a threshold beyond which the external world began with its adventures, its dangers and its discoveries. You stroll like a camel in this setting of miniature scenery trying not to overturn or trample anything.

Suddenly you are overtaken by a torpor which makes your limbs and brain heavy. You are a victim of the same disfunction of visual perception which used to seize you when you were an adolescent and later on more intermittently. This would generally happen when you were in a semi-somnolent state: you did not see things around you in their true proportions. Your body shrank and got smaller, if you stretched out your hand to reach what you were looking at, it used to seem to you smaller and further away, detached from your body. The walls of the room where you were lying and all the things in it moved away and grew smaller as if you were looking at them through the viewfinder of a camera. Even if you closed your eyes, the sensation would persist. Your brain was reduced to the size of an egg and your heart was no more than a valve which beat imperceptibly in your bird's breast. It was only when you got up and took a few

steps in the room, snorted, breathed deeply many times, that the sensation would gradually disappear.

It's in this condition that you arrive in the square of the district and find yourself in front of the house where you were born. You see yourself as a child, short-legged, with an enormous head which makes you look at things differently from the way they reveal themselves to objective memory. You are running with a swarm of children of your own age in the alleys of the neighbourhood. One of the nights of Ramadan when the evenings are warm and long and when the civil war between enemy neighbourhoods is in full swing. Infantile general-staffs are improvised. The tactics of war are planned and thwarted. Inventories are made of the leather belts available to the group. Only conventional arms are permitted to the belligerents. Rinds of watermelons and canteloupes are collected to be used to mine the no-man's-land in the district and to obstruct the forward march of the enemy. Ashes are collected in old metal barrels which are carried onto the balconies of houses overlooking the theatre of operations. At the right moment the ashes will be thrown over the heads of the attackers in order to blind them and to give an advantage in the hand-to-hand combat which will follow. Thick twine is gathered to be fastened to each side of the wall, a little above ground level, at the end of the darkest alley of the neighbourhood. It's here that the general staff will retreat while waiting for the last wave of attackers who have succeeded in surmounting other obstacles and who will get entangled by the hanging twine and be beaten in the hideout where they can be "finished off" with the belts.

150

The last oasis of your childhood is repopulated. Voices, faces, names rise up from this shipwrecked Atlantis. Bidous the one-legged beggar returns from his daily wandering, dressed in the same black overcoat which makes him look civilised in a bizarre kind of way. Mikou, simple soul, a man for any task bent under his burden, while singing songs with surrealistic words. Chahmout, hardened bachelor *cherif*, the district's Romeo, waiting for the dawn in order to appear beneath the window of his housewife Juliet – calling to her in his loud, hoarse butcher's voice. Si Abdellatif, another *cherif*, pot-bellied and idle, who liked the company of children and who used to tell them dirty stories and initiate them into the petty secrets of adulthood. Ould Daouïa, cross-eyed adolescent, weasel-faced orphan, poor and the chosen victim of other youths more privileged or stronger. Your playmates: Hat Roho, a boy with an angel's face with whom you endlessly engaged in quarrels and reconciliations. Loulidi, a mischievous devil with a thousand tricks in his bag. Hammad, an ill-tempered weakling and a cry-baby with a persecution complex.

Other faces. Other voices. Very soon the Ahl Touat leather works fill the district with their songs. Followed by travelling merchants, those who repair utensils, the scavengers . . .

The presence of your father brings you back to reality. You continue your walk. You try to struggle out of this crowded area of memory whose upper layers you have skimmed. You know that this quest has only just started, that you will have to come back to it again and again, not to unearth the fleeting images or far-off echoes, but to unravel the skein, take up the thread of the journey, give back significance and speech to a world whose fate has always been silence.

Bab Guissa. Once you have passed through the gate of the town, you find yourself in another world. You enter the city of the dead. But a particular city. You are not looking at a cemetery-esplanade where the graves need to be numbered or even the kind of cemetery-cesspit which gives the impression of a common grave. Here the graves are not stretched out to view separately. They are perched on small, neighbouring hills where they are lodged pointing downwards, laid out in corners, even at the edges of the ravines. Men here have made the most of the space, using the same ingenuity that the mountain peasants use to get the best out of their cultivated land and to site their dwellings. One would say that the plot of each grave has been chosen as a function of the landscape which it occupies.

The city of the dead is therefore another fresco in which you can read the harmony which men here share with the deceased and with the idea of their own death. You can easily feel the idea they have of eternity.

You clamber along the tarred path which leads to the graves higher up. Your father stops at the edge of the ravine and points out something below.

"You see, at the side of the saint's tomb, the large tomb right in the middle. It's there that your grand-father's laid to rest."

Yes. You can clearly see this large, solitary tomb, at the foot of the sanctuary's cupola. It's positioned like a sleeper stretched out in the sun.

Your father recites a prayer, in a low voice, before continuing on the path. You arrive at the foot of a small hill which has steps up it. You clamber up, walking among tombs.

You know now that your mother's grave is nearby. Your heart begins to beat more quickly. You can no longer contain your emotion. A strange feeling comes over you. Perhaps it arises from a common enough experience. You are a son who has lost his mother. But at this moment you see this simple fact differently. It's no longer an abstraction, situated and classified in categories by your thought-processes, integrated in the norms of universal behaviour, cast into the storeroom of commonplace sorrows. It becomes concrete, like the collision with a poem, that moment when the veil of the inexpressible is torn and gives way to a sudden surge of vision. Your feeling has the force of originality, of the new. It's like that of a child whose eyes are blinded by a great mystery and who reels around in a night of perplexity.

"It's here," says your father.

For a moment you think he has made a mistake. You don't see a single tomb but a rectangular platform, marked by a small wall, which is big enough for many graves.

"It's my family's tomb," your father explains. "Here's your mother's grave. Here lies your aunt. There, that's my place and your uncle's. And there's still some space left."

You draw closer to the space your father has pointed out. It's the first grave on the left. In the middle of the headstone there's an inscription which you read. Name, ancestry, date of death, a verse from the Koran. On the little wall you notice a small dried palm branch with a stone on it. Your father explains again:

"It's the *fqih* whom I've asked to come regularly to pray for her. Each time he leaves a sign of his visit."

A shiver goes up your spine. You let your hand rest on the headstone. You lift up your eyes. The two of you are alone in the graveyard. There are only a few sheep left by the shepherd which are in the process of browsing the thistles that grow among the tombs. The sun glares. There's not the least breeze. Up above, right at the top of the small hill, the tomb of a saint. You hear the voice of your father continuing his story:

"You know, we kept the news of your imprisonment from her. She was too ill to stand the shock. We had to tell her that you had gone abroad on a long journey. But in the last few months, she no longer believed it. She used to say that something had happened to you. You appeared to her several times in dreams and you were crying as you said good-bye to her. Her last words were for you. She blessed you for all eternity."

You turn your back on your father to hide your feelings. Without realising it, you have begun to caress the stone on the grave which no longer feels rough. Little by little, you realise that the caress is directed towards this most silent woman. You have an almost maternal feeling of stretching out your hand to her head and of caressing it with a spontaneous gesture of consolation.

You carefully wipe your eyes and turn back to your father.

He has lowered his head. You know that he has different feelings. He is familiarising himself with the second city of his journey. Then, without your being aware that this idea has taken root in you and is formed on your lips, you say to him:

"This space that's left here, I want you to keep it for me, father. My place has always been among you."

". . . I rise up after my insatiable night
electrified mass
finding again the use of perceptions faculties . . .
and then I dig return to the effort
denounce   denounce myself
I will never cease
unmask   unmask myself
I will never cease
invite   invite myself
I will never cease . . ."

7.

Free. Old salt of the prison seas. You are free. You have made progress since that afternoon when you felt the astonishment of a Columbus when the lookouts saw the coastline of the New World and cried: Land! Land!

The caravel of your prison voyage had begun to pitch beneath your feet. You had suddenly discovered that it was not an unidentified object bobbing endlessly in a blind trough of star-struck seas. It had finally taken you somewhere where you could berth, land, walk with your uncertain step of a convalescent who is hungrily rediscovering the taste of sunshine, in spite of its insipidity.

You experienced a first moulting, then a second. Each day on waking up you left in your bed an old skin which detached itself from you during a nightmare where you traversed one cave after another, cellars of executed criminals, where you came to a halt at the last moment at the edge of a precipice whose bottom you could not see. It was not a single paralysed or atrophied limb that you had to re-educate slowly through massage and gradual exercise. You needed time to fit together the two separated parts of your being, to stitch them together. You needed time to look, feel, hear and touch with the ordinary faculties of a man who can cross the road nonchalantly, stop at the edge of the sea, feel the trunk of a tree in the middle of the forest, caress a breast while the sap rises in him until it wets his lips. You needed time for the swarming clouds to become a crowd which strides up and down the cities, for the tumult to subside and to translate itself into differentiated voices, for the faces to take on life behind their masks of wax.

You re-learned the language of society. For weeks your bell never stopped ringing. One polite visit after another. You tried to carry out as well as you could your role as an object of curiosity, a man of extremities returned from a legendary journey. You opened the door yourself. You gave yourself to embraces and stereotyped formulas of best wishes. You replied while weighing your words to the questions which assailed you.

"How do you feel now?"

"Disoriented. I'll need time to recover."

"It must be quite something to find yourself outside again after so many years!"

"Yes. You have the feeling of being newly born with the brain of an old man, or an old man with the eyes of a baby."

"What most strikes you about the outside world?"

"The inflation of objects. To eat, for example, I used to have no need for anything except a mess-tin and a spoon. Now besides that, it's a whole battery of implements we use. I'm still astonished by the sight of a set-out table. This swarm of so-called useful objects by which we believe we are economising or making

158

things easier or more pleasant. There's also the rhythm of life, of movements which make me dizzy. To such an extent that I begin to envy the imaginary inhabitants of the moon who can live in a thinner atmosphere."

"Have you noticed changes in the country, a development?"

"Stagnation is meaningless. Everything moves and changes. But we still have to reach a correct understanding of the nature and the meaning of development. The old can put itself forward in new guises. And inversely the new can clothe itself in old shapes. Germination is by definition invisible."

"Do you mean to say by that that you yourself have not changed?"

"No. I am the image of this country. Let's say that I have learned a lot about myself, my abilities and my limitations, my revulsions and enthusiasms, about others as human contacts and as agents of change, about the world and the tricks of history. Leaving that aside, my heart is intact, even if it has been seriously ill-treated by imprisonment and dampness."

"You give the impression of being more gentle!"

"It's death and love which have deposited this ingredient in me."

"What are you doing now?"

"Letting things settle. Seeing more clearly into myself. Learning reality again. I shall, perhaps, write a book about all this experience."

"A collection of poems."

"No, an essay. What I used to call at one time an 'itinerary'."

"How do you account for these prison releases?"

"I certainly have some idea of what's going on. But we would have to look at other unusual aspects of current events if we really want to understand the underlying fundamentals of local political behaviour."

"What's your position now?"

"That of a wild animal which was caged and which has been released into a wildlife park."

Other meetings. Other conversations. A gallery of portraits. The person who preached for more than an hour without allowing you a chance to reply or to utter a word, castigating exploiters and exploited, putting everyone into the same bag of corruption and mediocrity in order to arrive at the conclusion that what this country needed was the man of destiny able to bring about the rule of a well-muscled justice, and who ended up by leaving you rejoicing in the interesting discussion he had had with you.

Another who launched himself into an analysis of the ideological ages through which all men pass, the last one, that of maturity and solid cohesion being the age of religion, and who only stopped speaking in order to gulp down large draughts of imported beer.

Yet another who made strenuous efforts to persuade you that you had given enough of yourself and that it was now the time for others in their turn to pay their dues to change.

You met again intellectuals, both embittered and complacent, agoraphobics who had retreated into their apartments festooned with safety chains, each one more impressive than the last, turning over projects that pre-dated your imprisonment, well settled into the generalised crises of arts and literature and into their own crisis of conscience.

You met up again with old acquaintances who offered you visiting cards covered with honours and telephone numbers. Eyes switched off. The dreams of youth buried. Technocrats, businessmen, transformed in the management of men and goods.

One day in the street you met a dinosaur from the university, holding in his hand a briefcase which gave him the air of being a James Bond at heart. He stopped you short, gripped you firmly by the arm and said like some *fqih* from a Koranic school:

"Well, I'm very happy for you. But I had told you. Do you remember what I said?"

No. Truly you did not remember the prophetic words of the university dinosaur.

"You can see now that I was right," he had replied, ignoring your response. Then he disappeared, as far as you were concerned, forever.

Other meetings. Other conversations. You were suffocated.

Then you were seized by a hunger for space. To leave. Turn your back on this ghetto which you knew only too well. Once more, break adrift.

You travelled the country in order to imbue yourself with the colours of the land, to look at men and women who followed their paths bent double under the burden of their needs and of the cancer of anger which gnawed at them. You went out to meet all the children who crossed your path. You smiled at them in the hope of seeing reborn on their lips, in the smouldering embers of their pupils, the sign by which they could reassure adults of the continuity and renewal of the force of life.

161

Casablanca, Marrakech, Tafilalet, Rif, Middle-Atlas.
You followed the green line of the Michelin guide
and the black broken line of poverty and the cudgel,
lost paths at the edge of which animals come to die of
hunger and thirst, men come to spit and to wait in the
rain for the miracle of the century.

Good God, what beauty, you would say to yourself,
and what ugliness! Your country was like a thin
gazelle chained up and smeared with dung.

You gradually took strength from contact with the
red land.

Autumn came. Then winter. Then summer.

The movement of the seasons was not marked
simply by variations in your metabolism, by pul-
sations which seared your senses to a lesser or
greater degree, the appearance or disappearance of
the swallow which made and unmade the spring. You
were seized by a turmoil of beginnings, of signs and of
emanations.

The wind rose. It was no longer the howling of a
wounded beast laying siege to the citadel, an icy blast
which sneaked back under the closed door or through
the open judas hole. It used to fill its cheeks like a
mythical giant stretched out over the town and blow
at the disorganised groups of clouds, lifting as it
passed hosts of dead leaves and rubbish, bending
double everything, whether human or vegetable, in
its way.

The rains came. Not the distracted tapping on the
cell roof, the savage misery of the rain falling on the
deserted yard. These were violent, brief storms,
beating the house, washing the heart and the lungs of
the town, creating a large funnel in the throat of the

earth in order to pour into it the long awaited downpour.

The sun came out of its rusty, concrete box, left the avenues to cultivated plants, leaped over carnivorous walls to grow and multiply there where the horizon emphasised with a torquoise line the threshold of eternity, to mirror itself in lakes, capricious gulleys, in the sand dunes of saffron yellow, or the carved face of the rocky outcrops, somewhere in the valley of the Dadès or the gorges of Todrha.

Little by little you recovered from your astonishments. You rediscovered reflexes that you thought you had lost forever. To drive a car, to type, look at your watch to see the time, get out money to pay, open a newspaper without paying attention to where you were ... You fitted your appointments, your shopping and your work into the unity of conventional time which is a day of twenty-four hours. Your astonishment bumped less every day against the rock of realities and good sense. Already there was memory and forgetting. Your new life already had an age.

Then there were the great questions. Not that they had been absent after the first steps you had taken during the starry night of your deliverance. From that instant you had said to yourself: Look at me, returned again to the multiple body from which I had been snatched. How shall I find again the land and the people? How shall I create again with my hands their fertility? But now, you had seen. The earth had turned. The rivers had recovered their normal courses. The social puzzle had been fitted together. Nevertheless you had a private belief that the

163

inevitable question "What is to be done?" could not be posed as nakedly as before. As soon as it was formulated, a host of other questions arose, not raising doubts or rejecting it, but creating qualifications, putting it into an incontrovertible background. The questions were: "What was I and what have I become? What have we done? What was the part played by error and blindness? What's now left to care for, the most valuable part of ourselves, of our dreams, the most valuable of that for which sacrifices were made, blood shed? What part did we reproduce in ourselves of the monstrosity we struggled against? What illusions did we take into ourselves in our hunting to death of the dominant illusions? And of all those words which served as sign-posts, traffic lights, which were the counterfeits and which were those authenticated by practice, the pitiless play of truth and error? What did we repeat and only repeat like impressionable parrots and what did we revitalise, create and transfigure by our own lucidity, our mastery of reality in both its individual and its universal aspects? Why did this great gathering together of the wretched which was brought about for an assault on the reign of barbarity transform itself into a myriad of petty sects ruled by the law of splitting, cultivating if not contempt then hatred for other comrades each of whom felt sure he had the correct line and that he was under a flag which was a more lively and more proletarian red than that of others? Sects where the spirit of hierarchy, multi-faceted dogmatism, abhorrent subjectivism returned with a vengeance exactly like that against which they had warred and which they had thought they had

164

beaten. Sects each of which was more hostile towards the other than towards the bloody Molochs who continued to steal the harvests and to devour each year the virgins of the community . . ."

You had opened the sluice-gates to questions. And the surge was now out of your control. You did not try to impede it. You had arrived at the stage where one can no longer stop, make a half-turn, argue from the perplexity and confusion that these questions could arouse to come back to them later, when the time might be more fitting, when you had taken every precaution so that you would not find yourself in the position of someone who is swimming against the tide, foolishly revealing the wounds and the defects which ought to be kept hidden, washing dirty linen in public and making revelations which could give an advantage to the other side, the enemy.

You would ignore the logic of the respectable citizen who is suffering from a shameful disease, but who refuses to go to the doctor for fear of what everyone will say. Besides, you know very well that these questions surround you, that the mud which clung to them spattered you as well. You were not trying to whitewash yourself or get out of the fight, rest on your laurels as a combatant. You knew that your truth had its price. Like the truth of a whole phase of the struggle which was nevertheless part of that heritage of enlightenment thanks to which this country's dispossessed would finally find a way out of the maze of shadows which they tread with tireless steps.

In formulating these questions you believed you could hear a fraternal voice which contradicted you.

And this voice said: "The proletarian revolution must carry forward and has already carried forward the historical need of humanity for the full development of man. This is why, for example, I cannot forget that the red flag – 'red with the workers' blood' – bears indelibly, also in bright red, the blood of Bukharin and we must never forget that, lest we make the same mistake . . . "

You agreed, but also added that the blood of Bukharin was not just a smudge, a mistake which could be overcome by the simple ritual of criticism and self-criticism in a meeting. The order that it should be shed had already been inscribed in certain conceptions of that instrument which should have brought the workers to power, realised human justice on earth, abolished inequalities, given to man, to all men now equal, their own creative genius. It was already inscribed in the process of that astonishing metamorphosis during the course of which the destroyers of oriental despotism incorporated into themselves its essence, its fatal poison, from the instant when they became the masters of a smattering of power.

The instrument. The dilemma. Is it not, in every place and every circumstance, the concentrated image of the society which it dreams of, of the social and human relations which it will create? From that moment on, the question does not pose itself simply in Shakespearian terms: to be or not to be. Whether the instrument determines the process or the process, the instrument. The questions which arise could be the following: What kind of instrument? Who does it belong to and for whom? Made for what and for what futures so that one can be sure they will not be simple transfers or caricatures of those already in existence here and there and which one cannot analyse in terms of regression or progress without falling into looseness of language.

Yes brother. We have not finished, deep down in ourselves, with oriental despotism. You know that. And I challenge you to tell me that your flesh and your conscience are not still wounded. And to get rid of this black blood of a spreading cancer, it's no use having recourse to valium or the aspirin of change in continuity, it will be necessary to batter away at the hard rock of reality, rise up against the manuals, stain their immaculate covers with our dirty hands. It will be necessary to call ourselves into question. Not nicely, with that spirit of compassion for our youthful follies, our mis-understandings, our limits fixed and signalled by the limitations and immaturity of the time, but violently, from the soles of our feet to the tops of our heads as we say in Arabic, crush and break the idols of our own complacency. Erupt from the other end of the tunnel of the Cave of Ideas. Not so that we can bask in calm seas but so that we can take up the staff of pilgrimage, take up again the way of the cross, and to do this we shall have to bring in not Justice and the anonymous just, but the hideous body of the Templars of dispossession.

The voice would return, bearing other dilemmas. You seemed to hear this exchange about human rights, europocentrism, separation of ways. The voice would say:

"There's one here who says, about these rights, which is the most fundamental, the most sacred, that which determines the others (while not being sufficient in itself)? Which is this sacred right that Western intellectuals can allow themselves the luxury of forgetting because for *them*, for the citizens of *their* countries, it could be now relatively easily acquired (leaving aside the risk of a world war, it's true, but they also forget that). The right is the *right to life*, and above all, the *right to life of children*. Here we know the position not only with regard to infant mortality, malnutrition, but also of the disgrace which is the reality for so many children in working-class districts in large towns, for example, sniffing the exhaust fumes of buses to help them forget their misery and hunger.

"This situation is widespread for what is called the Third World.

"Here is what is written in a report of the W.H.O. which studies the weight of infants at birth: 'In every country and in every social class, weight is the primary factor which determines the chances of survival for the newly born ... Even in the case of those who survive, the consequences of a low birth weight are the following: respiratory troubles, hypo-thermia, an increased susceptibility to illnesses, central nervous system problems, hearing and sight problems ... It is necessary in order to assure those infants a normal life to have frequent recourse to clinical methods which exceed the economic and technological resources for most of the developing countries.'

"For it is precisely here that the drama is taking

place: in 1979 out of a total of 112 million live births, 21 million of the newly born weighed less than 2,500 grams. Each year 200,000 children die here. 200,000 children each year! That means 550 children die every day, 23 children every hour, 1 child every two and a half minutes.

"It's here therefore that one must locate the problem, in the first instance for conscience's sake, but also for all those who seek a way out of death and shame and for whom, whether we wish it or not, we are the bearers of hope. To fold our arms because the model and the means which lead to this end are 'impure', that's called failing to help a person in danger."

You thought about your own opinion on the matter. Was it just a matter of replying? Of contributing yourself as one of the poles in an artificial contradiction? You knew very well that was not the case. You had already responded to this question, not as one might reply to a philosophical debate in a Sartrean dilemma, but in "real life", heart and soul, and with no stinting in what you gave. And your reply changed the course of your life, of your practice, of your feelings. It took you a long way, a thousand miles from the poisonous circles of calculations and petty-mindedness. It took you far, so far that it was impossible for you to locate, somewhere behind you, the point of no return that you had left at a certain moment in your journey, without even noticing it.

Yes brother. If you could only doubt it! This belt of communal graves of children condemned to death from birth is well and truly the boundary which makes us men with the same compulsion, ·

holds us to the same line, lookouts in the same trench, even when we are not side by side. It's the demarcation line which separates us and will always separate us from the guard dogs, the birds of ill omen, the harnessed horses (whether blinkered or not) who agree to turn undisturbed the water wheel of petty reforms, from the Cassandras who give thanks for each historical change, ill-at-ease in their impotence and prostituted realism, and who return to the easy bosoms of their first loves. This belt which cuts the country, the towns, the villages into two incredibly unequal parts, which extends like a disfiguring wall between those who are judged useful and those who are left out of account (mouths, lives, lands). This is our lighthouse on the mountainous sea where we fight against the wildness of the elements and our own weaknesses.

So brother, watch out for those words which sound like a gong announcing the irretrievable. We are no longer in the time of fiery speeches that can set flame to the country, of those instant analyses whose conclusions are already programmed into their premises. We are no longer in the time of casting out seeds to every wind that blows. We are neither in the time of epic nor of tragedy. Plenty of our gods turned out to be mortal and corruptible. They can no longer fulfil in our daily drama the role of stagehands or prompters. Our stage is now bare. So are our gods and so are we. And I say so much the better for that. Our words are finally going to be able to express us faithfully, not our costumes or accessories.

Do you realise how long it took us to verify what

was being said by those sacrilegious demons who had dared to raise their hands against the idols of our new Olympus? And when we lent an ear to the siren song and cautiously approached the shrine of our idols we discovered that they had already been overturned.

So brother, watch out for words and actions whose roots you cannot trace, that's the first thing. Hope is a hard vocation. It's a work of an eternally anxious love. It's not an industry whose tool should be the blow-lamp of anathema and exclusion. Truth will never be an object of monopoly, nor will suffering. Don't fold your arms, you say. Yes. But don't close your eyes either, or your heart, or brain, if I can take this figure of speech to its extreme. So that, when armed with this multiple clarity we carry help to those in danger, we will know how to administer first aid, and we will not make a mistake about the medicine, nor carry out any remedies which might prove fatal to the victims. Furthermore, this image of "helpism" seems inopportune to me and dangerous, based as it is on the old idea of the lover of justice, which we combat in theory but produce and reproduce ceaselessly in practice.

So then, to be responsible, what does this mean in the war of attrition and tactics in which we have already lost a few battles? It's above all to know how to learn the lessons of our defeats, question our experience, re-read it in the cross-fire of obstinate facts, learn to doubt, verify, put everything in question instead of being content with assimilating and confirming what has been tested in other climates, know the local terrain, the position of minefields like shimmering mirages, penetrate the enemy's strategy in its stagnant and its dynamic aspects, know how to evaluate our forces at each stage, get rid of this warlord mentality which divides and scatters our ranks. But really, really, I would so much like not to have to remember and repeat that all this is impossible unless we have succeeded, against all odds, in keeping intact the sacred fire of our dreams, this rational and ineradicable faith in a future where men will overcome the original sin of this world, will restore peace, make of our planet a natural satellite sending out to near and distant galaxies the deepest message of humanity, the love of life, the love of love, the love of everything that is given.

You had opened the sluice-gate to questions. And the surge was now out of your control. What price would you have to pay now for having done so? You thought you could already hear the mephistophelian chuckles of every kind of manichean, those who fomented public gossip and who were not lacking in the means necessary to mutilate your ideas, while keeping what suited them, what they wanted to keep, retain or let go after taking them out of context and out of their logical sequence. On one side, there would doubtless arise the cry of destroyer, denier, and on the other of irredentism, congenital extremism, utopian fervour. But you are not frightened. You know that your cry is a hard bone to swallow for those vultures who attack their victim before he has breathed his last. You know that there is no one with enough power to destroy the irreducible kernel of your identity which you succeeded in keeping in the worst times of your ordeal when you were balanced on the tightrope of an absolute dilemma and when pain seized the bloody football of your brain, when your body was no more than a swollen appendage. No one will be able to destroy the irreducible kernel of your identity. Neither the disbelieving friend nor the furious enemy. Still less the jaundiced smile of the gentlemen of language. You have caught up with your liberty at the furthest crossroads of its seriousness. You have grown, both in age and stature, out of squabbling and individual resentments. You have grown out of the epoch of initiatory exams and stage fright in front of the professors of conscience. Above all else, you know you are the repository of an inheritance fed with blood, kneaded and steeped in the crucible of struggle, of advances and retreats, of splendid solidarities at the hands of those who never fail.

And to loop the loop, here you are back in place, a necessary passage which could not have been left out of your itinerary. The river has subsided. Some moored boats slowly sway in the light swell of this late afternoon. You lift your eyes. And what you see first is the mane of the palm tree stretched out in the wind like a faded banner. The high walls repainted in white stretch around the small hill on which is set the citadel of exile. The watchtowers spring up in turn, aiming their searchlights, showing off the barrels of their guns. The terrace of the fortifications emerges, riddled with holes where pigeons roost. A subdued noise rises from the prison. You think you can hear the clack of large keys turning the locks, the squeaking of the trolley wheels on which the orderlies bring the evening's soup. You think you are reliving your last conversation with the palm tree before going to your cell. Set in the middle of the yard. You talk to the tree and it responds. Two fools ruminating on the meaning of life and death, on the irrationality of a world ruled by the species of reasonable men. The first star pierces the narrow rectangle of the sky. It begins to shine timidly, just above the top of the palm. It speaks to you in its turn and you respond. You are like two children lost in the jungle who hold hands to ward off the infinite, the overwhelming mystery of the universe, the wild beating of their hearts.

The siren of a boat sounds behind you. Other sirens reply. You turn round and, for an instant, you have the impression that you are going back to your cell, replacing the tin with your pathetic evening's ration, waiting for the warder to come and double-lock your door before you lie on your mattress, open your eyes on the screen of your ceiling and project onto it the film of the day. You take a few steps in the direction of the river. On the horizon a large red-orange sun sinks slowly beneath the agitated kaleidoscope of the waves. You remember the story of the little girl who became a sun. And this large, flamboyant orange seems to measure itself against the nearness of the citadel of exile, put its force of dramatic suggestion against this promontory where confiscated bodies and languages are turned each day into an airy song which climbs, reaches out, rejoins and swells the gigantic plaint rising from our earth and which you are sure will reach, light-year after light-year, to

174

all that is born to awareness in the universe, manifestations of life and intelligence, humanities from fertile ages and cities of peace, clear blood, soft hands like the fontanelles of babies, deep and readable eyes and repositories of smiles.

Free. Old salt of the prison seas. If you are now free, it's because you will carry this citadel, for the rest of your life, engraved on your heart.

Epilogue

At the close of this book, see what other torments await you. The steam-roller that you have managed to release to vanquish silence is in revolt. You read again at one sitting what you have written. And you feel disoriented. This very essay has become a mystery to you. How did all this start? How did the power of selection function with regard to situations and events arbitrarily promoted to the role of being significant elements which could make more sense than others? According to what criteria have you chosen the principal and the secondary, the objective and the subjective? More perplexing still, how will this offering be received by those who did not share your experience, who have only the vaguest idea lodged in them by the cinema or bits of reading? How will it be received by those who shared it with you and who still have it like a live flame every day in their flesh and their spirits? Have you really succeeded in resolving the paradox of the blind painter, the deaf musician and the paralysed ballerina? What exactly have you attacked and what defended? What silence, what silences have you challenged in releasing haphazardly your urge to speak? What image have you created of yourself and of your vindicated body?

Pride, humility? Artlessness, clarity? Stubbornness, realism?

More worrying still, this YOU that you consecrated as hero or chief character, who will fall into the trap of believing that it has anything to do with an individual? Will it not be understood as WE? What then have you put of yourself into the mouths of others and what of others into your own mouth? And with what justification?

Yet again, are these questions only dictated by your habit of doubt? Other torments await you.

You are not one of those official writers for whom a book is simply an object in a contract which connects them with the Establishment of the writing business. You do not plan. You do not practice the economy of materials, you do not carefully ration the sources of your inspiration so that enough will be left for further harvests. You are a kind of visionary of the art of writing. You put your entire self into what you write because you know that the flood could arrive at any moment, and, without being too dramatic, you know that the instant when you are writing, you are perhaps in the process of editing your spiritual will.

You know also that whatever the variations in tone, of subjects broached, of genre used, you in fact endlessly draft the same book, come back to its burden, frequent the same places in the same violent journey, of scalp-hunting, of visions, of passions known and unknown, of truths marked by the warning light of error and the upheaval of one's existence. Your concern is not the same as that of those who build the pyramids or the Brasilias of the spirit. You were and will always remain a sower of the seeds of rebellion, a potholer of origins, of rough and ready accessories. Water-diviner for the greatest source of life. A walking seismograph in the jungle of the twentieth century.

You know what you are and you proclaim unequivocally: A FOOL FOR HOPE.

From this came action.

You speak to those who can still hear the cry of man.

About the translator: JACQUELINE KAYE received her M.Phil. from London University and is a Lecturer in the Department of Literature at the University of Essex. Besides her work as a teacher and translator, she has recently completed a critical study of Francophone Algerian and Moroccan writers to be published by Routledge.